"Detective Cagan's Really Too Good-looking For A Man,"

Noelle's sister persisted, watching from the window as Cagan strode toward the house. "Black eyes, black hair... He needs a haircut, or at least a comb. He always looks like he just climbed out of some woman's bed."

"Eva!" Noelle blushed.

"Well, he does. Lucky woman. And that wrinkled raincoat needs to go to the dry cleaner. And that tie... But even from this distance, I can't see why you even date Beaumont, Noelle."

"I told you I don't want to talk about Garret Cagan ever again. Besides, I'm probably going to marry Beau. Everybody says he's perfect for me."

"What do they know?"

"At least Beau's not like some wild animal that bites your hand off every time you try to do something nice for him."

"You're like me, *chère*. We've always had a way with wild animals...."

Dear Reader:

Welcome! You hold in your hand a Silhouette Desire – your ticket to a whole new world of reading pleasure.

As you might know, we are continuing the *Man of the Month* concept through to May 1991. In the upcoming year look for special men created by some of our most popular authors: Elizabeth Lowell, Annette Broadrick, Diana Palmer, Nancy Martin and Ann Major. We're sure you will find these intrepid males absolutely irresistible!

But Desire is more than the *Man of the Month*. Each and every book is a wonderful love story in which the emotional and sensual go hand-in-hand. A Silhouette Desire can be humourous or serious, but it will always be satisfying.

For more details please write to:

Jane Nicholls
Silhouette Books
PO Box 236
Thornton Road
Croydon
Surrey
CR9 3RU

ANN MAJOR

SCANDAL'S CHILD

Silhouette Desire

Originally Published by Silhouette Books
a division of
Harlequin Enterprises Ltd.

First published in Great Britain in 1990 by Silhouette Books, Eton House, 18-24 Paradise Road, Richmond, Surrey TW9 1SR

© Ann Major 1990

Silhouette, Silhouette Desire and Colophon are Trade Marks of Harlequin Enterprises B.V.

ISBN 0 373 57957 8

22 – 9009

Made and printed in Great Britain

LETTER FROM ANN MAJOR:

The forbidden has always held great allure for me, so I was intrigued with Noelle Martin, who first appeared in *Wilderness Child*. Noelle had loved a forbidden man and had run away to Australia to forget him. But Garret Cagan was unforgettable.

Noelle grew up in a pillared mansion in lush Louisiana bayou country. Garret grew up in a shack. Her family wanted her to marry a gentleman banker. Garret Cagan was a cop.

I set this story in Louisiana because I once lived in bayou country, and I find its brooding atmosphere hauntingly beautiful.

I hope that you enjoy reading this book as much as I enjoyed writing it.

Other Silhouette Books by Ann Major

This book is dedicated to Tara Gavin.
She has been not only my editor and creative partner
but a friend.

I am deeply grateful to her
for her talent, her kindness and her patience.

And a special thank you to Luther Kaim.

Prologue

Outside the Jackson ranch house, the sun was blazing. It was only the beginning of June, but in south Texas, it felt like high summer.

A black horse ran wild and free in the golden pasture. Noelle Martin glanced out the window and longed to be on that horse, riding bareback through those high grasses, her red hair streaming in the warm wind.

Instead she felt stiff and hot in her tight satin gown, constrained by the formalities of wedding etiquette. A wisp of tulle at her shoulder scratched her every time she moved. Across the room her still-beautiful and still-scandalous mother was embarrassing sedate Papa as usual by drinking too much champagne and dazzling every male from the age of eight to eighty.

Noelle felt caught in a snarl of indecision. Should she go to Europe to buy antiques for Mama's shop? Or home to Louisiana as Papa wished?

For two years Noelle had stayed away—to forget Garret Cagan and all that had gone wrong between them. To forget the baby they'd lost and his son, Louis, whom she had loved as her own. Could she really go back without constantly thinking of Garret and all that he'd meant to her?

Noelle had gone to Australia and stayed there for two years trying to forget him, but he had proven unforgettable. Stamped onto her heart and mind was the hateful memory of his wild, rebel-without-a-cause aura, of his devil-dark good looks—his black hair, his equally black eyes, his tall muscular body. They'd grown up together, although he had come from a swamp shack and she from a white-columned mansion. Garret had grown up hard on a diet of poverty and adversity. She'd been nurtured and spoiled from the moment she'd toddled out of her cradle in pursuit of him.

But now, just the thought of Garret stirred the old restlessness deep inside her.

The black horse galloped past the house with wild abandon. Noelle looked away, no longer able to bear the sight of him. He reminded her of another horse, of another time, of a stolen moment when she'd been a girl, riding bareback behind Garret with the soft sunlight filtering through the dense cypress trees. As they'd galloped past blooming dogwood and purple violets along the bayou's edge, the woods had seemed magical, free, and—most of all—their very own. She'd clutched her lover tightly, as if to hold on to him and that brief idyllic time together forever. Noelle's eyes misted. She felt choked with conflicting emotions.

"It's time to throw the bouquet," Mercedes shouted, snapping Noelle back to reality.

"Bridesmaids and all the rest of you single girls, the bride's in the foyer!"

A ripple of interest whispered through the crowd.

"Sounds like the bridegroom is getting impatient."

It was the first Saturday in June, and it was Jess and Tad Jackson's wedding day. The Jackson ranch house, the dazzling chandelier, the wedding party—everyone and everything was decorated sumptuously in purple satin. The house was filled with familial warmth and happiness, the sounds of laughter, the sound of crystal champagne glasses clinking together. Members of the Texas aristocracy mingled with beloved ranch hands. Upstairs the nursery was filled with Jackson babies. The happiness of the bride and groom had infected the Texas crowd with a mood of joyous expectancy.

Everyone except the maid of honor. In the midst of such happiness, Noelle felt strained. She stood apart from the cluster of excited bridesmaids. This was the sort of wedding *Grand-mère* and Papa had always longed for her to have. They wanted her to forget Garret. They wanted her to marry Beaumont Vincent. Afterward, she would live in Beau's grand mansion and be the queen of its cold, formal rooms. Together they would be the toast of New Orleans society. She had been trained to be the perfect hostess, the perfect society matron. Beau belonged to her world.

Noelle forced a smile and tried to convince herself that the opulent Texas ranch house was not a gilded prison, that the aristocratic guests were not her jailers and that her friend's wedding was not a cruel reminder of her own doom.

The other women were fidgeting hopefully at the prospect of catching the bridal bouquet. Noelle felt tense and faint in her tight dress. Her glorious hair was the only thing about her that was not contained. It had come loose from its amethyst-and-pearl clips and streamed down her back in a wildly cascading tumble of scintillating bronze-and-gold flame.

She backed into the shadows. If only there was somewhere she could hide. But she was hemmed in by wedding guests. By Jess.

All loves did not end in weddings and happiness. Not if one loved unwisely. The image of Garret's swarthy face rose in Noelle's mind. He'd lived his life on the edge so long, he would never be completely tamed.

With an effort she pushed thoughts of Garret out of her mind. She had come today only for Jess. Sweet, stubborn, triumphant Jess. Jess, who'd defied her fiancé and befriended Noelle in Australia. Noelle was determined not to do anything to spoil Jess's wedding day.

She forced herself to concentrate on her bossy friend, who was gathering her lavender-embossed wedding gown edged in embroidered lace and smiling radiantly up at Tad as she moved away from the other women. In that last second before Jess turned her back and prepared to toss her bouquet, her brilliant dark gaze met Noelle's.

"No..." Noelle pleaded silently. "No...*mon Dieu*... don't throw it to... Not to me, *chère*." But even as she uttered her secret prayer, she knew Jess would do exactly as she pleased.

From the first, Jess had been determined to fling Noelle back into the frantic current of life. "You came to Australia to run away forever," Jess had said, "but I won't let you. You're going home where you belong—to *him*."

To *him*... Never.

But irony of ironies, here she was. So very near Louisiana. So near Garret and... Louis.

Her family still hated Garret. She told herself she hated him, too. Not that *he* could ever forgive any of them. And there was Louis, his darling golden-haired boy whom she loved as her own. Noelle closed her eyes, dark lashes fluttering with pain.

Jess threw the bouquet.

Squeals of excitement from the other women rang in the foyer.

Noelle opened her eyes. The bouquet was coming toward her. "No..."

Noelle grabbed the newel post and glanced frantically upstairs.

From the landing, Tad Jackson glared down at her like an ominous giant. His great male body blocked any chance of escape to the deserted upper regions of the ranch house.

With horror Noelle watched the bouquet sailing high into the air in slow motion and then fall straight toward her.

White blossoms and purple ribbons grazed her arm, her gown; the bouquet bounced off her hand and fell to the ground. A fragile cloud of sweet perfume from the flowers enveloped her.

Everyone in the room was staring at her.

Then a purple dynamo of satin skirts and frilled petticoats dived toward Noelle and pounced on the bouquet. It was Lizzie, Tad's little girl. She was bright and sparkling—as loving by nature as Louis. Lizzie's hair ribbons had come loose and hung crazily over her brow as she beamed up at Noelle.

Lizzie lifted the flowers to Noelle. "It's yours, Noelle!"

Noelle, who'd always loved children, wanted to shrink from the eager face, from the tiny outstretched hands filled with blossoms.

The flowers made Noelle feel vaguely ill and strange, as if they were funereal blossoms instead of softly scented wedding flowers.

"No... Give it to someone else."

The other girls were pressing close, clamoring for her to throw the bouquet again. Then, as always, Jess seized command, calmed the women, gently took the bouquet from Lizzie and placed it into Noelle's cold, shaking hands. "Take them, darling," she whispered.

Noelle smiled stiffly. "You shouldn't have..."

In a louder tone that floated to every corner in the room, Jess said, "Seek your destiny." Then she kissed Noelle's temple.

Noelle felt trapped. She could do nothing but stay where she was. She could do nothing but watch Jess rush up the stairs to the man she loved.

Noelle had never felt more alone, more lost.

She looked helplessly at the white flowers. What she wanted was to have what Jess had—to become the bride of the man she loved and the mother of his sweet child.

Noelle no longer saw the flowers. They were blurred. For her such a marriage would never be possible.

She tried to imagine Beaumont's face.

Instead she saw Garret's.

In her mind's eye she saw her purple satin gown discarded in a heap upon the soft ground beside a brown bayou. Her sparkling amethyst clips lay on top of that crumpled gown. She was wild and gloriously free, running along secret, never-forgotten paths. Garret was racing after her, but she didn't let him catch her until she had reached their secret place.

She caught her breath.

Mon Dieu!

She could never never go back. It was impossible for her to be indifferent to Garret.

And yet Papa said *Grand-mère* was not well, that she had never completely recovered from her stroke and seemed to be failing gradually.

"It's you she misses, *chère*," Mama had said as well. "You kept her young. For so many years we thought she was invincible. But she's not. She's dying of a broken heart."

How well Noelle knew that feeling.

One

A bullet ricocheted against the second story of the brick building. There were screams from the crowd. A pregnant woman fainted. Everyone else scrambled for cover.

"Man, this is better than Mardi Gras!" a bystander shouted before a patrolman ordered him on his way.

Another bullet splintered a brick.

"He ain't much of a shot, no."

"Do you think he'll kill her?"

"Maybe." The single word held exhilaration. "He ain't no soft-shell crab, him! He's a hard man, yes. He robbed a bank on Canal Street."

"And now he's holed up in that shop. The Martin girl, Noelle, who owns it is his hostage. He's been shooting out of that window up there."

The window was darkly shuttered and laced with black grill.

"Okay, people! Move it. Before somebody gets hurt!" shouted a fat cop in blue.

It was a cold November afternoon—bleak and misty. Royal Street was jammed with a dozen police cars, their lights blinking like fiery diadems, their radios squawking with static and calls. The sidewalks that ran beside the expensive antique shops kept filling with gawkers despite police efforts to keep them clear.

On the edge of the craziness, away from the other policemen, Detective Garret Cagan stood apart, a tense and solitary figure. He was lean and tall, well over six feet. Although his leather jacket protected his broad shoulders, his black head was hatless in the drizzle. His dark face was grim as he speculated on the pattern of the bullet holes high above his head in the brick wall.

Something was wrong about those holes; something was wrong about the entire setup. He could feel it in his bones. And he blamed Noelle.

He thought that if it hadn't been for her, he would be miles from the French Quarter, miles from her exclusive antique shop, on his way home now. Out in his pirogue maybe—alone on his slow, snake-dark bayou. Instead he was standing on city pavement in the rain with his stomach knotting in fear.

Redheads! They were a different breed!

Especially rich ones who thought they owned the world. Especially Noelle Martin. She was impossible, fickle, spoiled, unpredictable. She was the most supremely maddening woman Garret had ever encountered. And he'd known her for most of his life. He'd been five years old when she'd crawled out of her cradle and stormed into the center of his life. From that moment, she'd done nothing except cause turmoil and grief for him.

Once. No, *twice*, he'd made the worst mistake of his life by falling in love with her. Or perhaps he'd always loved her. She'd broken his heart, nearly broken him. He was still paying a bitter price for that emotion. She was the one woman he was determined to avoid.

And yet… Ever since they'd been kids growing up in the lush bayou country an hour outside of New Orleans, every time she got into trouble, he'd always wound up saving her. He'd saved her when she was three and had tried to pet that gator and had lost her balance and fallen into the bayou with him. When she was five she'd been playing with matches in her playhouse and set it on fire. Garret had barely gotten her out in time, and then the Martins had blamed him for setting the fire that had devoured not only the playhouse, but a live oak and nearly Martin House itself. When she was eight she'd climbed a trellis to peep through the shutters of her parents' bedroom while they'd been indulging in an amorous nap. The trellis had come loose, and Garret had caught her when she and the jasmine and the splintering wood came tumbling down on top of him. Noelle had run off. Senator Wade Martin had stumbled outside, wrapped in a towel, his face purple with rage and discovered Garret in the coils of jasmine. Garret had taken the rap for that, too.

Even on that last terrible night two years ago, Garret had tried everything he knew to save her. To save their baby. *His* baby. The child she hadn't wanted.

Garret shifted his gaze from its intense scrutiny of the puzzling bullet holes higher to the window from which the shots had been fired.

For a frozen fraction of a second he saw her framed there—her beautiful white face, her mass of red hair, her immense eyes, wide with terror. He'd seen that look before—too many times—and it was her face, not his dead wife's, that he'd dreamed of every night for the past two years.

Noelle—vital, alive, incorrigible. The same Noelle who'd followed him everywhere in the bayou until she'd come to know it almost as well as he had.

Only now she was even lovelier than he remembered. Seeing her, he felt a sudden overwhelming sensation. It was like an impact, like being struck a crushing blow. First he was cold. Then his skin seemed seared by flame. Something hard and unbreakable was flying to pieces inside him. He had fought to forget her, but in that moment he knew he never would.

Noelle jumped back from the glass, or was yanked back, but he knew she'd seen him.

As quickly as it had happened, the moment was over, but it made his stomach coil in a fresh spasm of terror. His palms were damp; his heart was thudding. The narrow walls of the street were closing in upon him like a trap. He had to do something. He knew he was close to panic.

Noelle was up there, in danger, helpless, a prisoner at the mercy of some lunatic with a gun.

The wild desperation wouldn't leave Garret.

Damn her. He couldn't take another second of this. She always made him crazy—as crazy as she was. He had to get her out.

Garret glanced at the darkened shop. At the fire escape, the windows, the doors. She'd never been worth all that she'd cost him. Never.

The captain would can him for disobeying orders.

It didn't matter.

Somehow he had to get inside. Before it got dark. Before she did something wild and it was too late.

Damn her for always doing this to him.

It never occurred to him to blame the bank robber for this chaos instead of Noelle. He knew her too well. She'd been the rich little girl with the penchant for trouble in the big plantation house, Martin House, that bordered his land. She'd been high and mighty—too good for him—until she got herself into some scrape. He'd been shy and unsure then, the cook's son who'd done odd jobs around the place. His brawn had been put to work toting fifty-pound fertilizer sacks, hefting chain saws to cut down dead trees. But he'd been dazzled by the little girl with the bright, corkscrew curls, whose idolatrous gaze followed him when nobody was looking, the same little girl who'd stolen his pirogue once and gotten herself lost in the swamp. Her family had been ill with anxiety until Garret had found her and brought her safely home. Then, as always, they'd blamed him, especially her grandmother—for having left his pirogue where Noelle could get it.

He knew how crazy Noelle could drive a person, how unpredictable she could be when some cockeyed notion got into her head. There'd been a score of people in that bank who'd minded their own business during the robbery. Not Noelle. He'd gotten the story straight from a dozen witnesses that she'd tackled the bank robber as he was running out, taken his money and bolted with it. Only the guy had caught her. Now he was holed up with her in her shop.

The fat patrolman whispered something into Garret's ear.

Garret's black eyes grew even blacker. The line of his mouth narrowed as his hand touched the holster of the semiautomatic he wore concealed beneath his leather jacket.

"She what?" Normally Garret's voice was a slurred Cajun drawl. The two-word question was an explosion.

"She said she won't come out, Detective Cagan. The guy said he'd let her go half an hour ago, but she's afraid we'll shoot him."

"Tell her—"

Another bullet zipped into the brick wall above Garret and sent bits of mortar and brick sprinkling down into his black hair.

"Dammit!"

Garret and the other officer dived for cover. Again Garret saw that the bullet was too high. Way too high. For the last half hour, the bullets had been high like that.

Suddenly, using the instincts of a cop who'd been on the street a long time, Garret knew.

He was almost sure. On the offhand chance he was wrong, he grabbed his shotgun out of his pickup and racked a shell into the chamber. "Forget trying to tell her anything, Johnson. I'm going in. Alone."

"What about backup?"

"Alone."

"But the captain said—"

"To hell with the captain. Give me five minutes. Ten max! If I don't have her out by then, come after me."

Garret's rugged broad-shouldered form was loping lithely across the pools of water in the narrow street when a gray Mercedes braked to a stop behind the police cars. A tall blond man jumped out. He was elegant, effete, not like the common rough-and-tumble crowd who kept pushing at the police barricades. Not like Garret.

The man's thin unlined patrician features were those of someone who'd never done an honest day's work in his life. His slicked-back hair was immaculate and perfect—too perfect. The instant he recognized Garret, his pale blue eyes frosted with a layer of ice. He picked his way over the barricades, lifting his legs delicately. Then he hurried toward

Garret, tiptoeing across dank puddles, barking orders and questions with the arrogance of a man who'd been born so rich he thought that it was his inalienable right to boss everyone, especially Cagan.

"Cagan! What the hell are you doing here? If something happens to Noelle, I'll personally guarantee you'll never work in New Orleans again. I'll close Mannie's down. You won't even be able to get a job on a garbage truck."

Garret stopped and propped his shotgun on his shoulder. There was the glint of amused contempt in his dark eyes. It was harder than hell to get Beaumont so mad he'd yell like a common street fighter. Garret knew because he'd tried often enough as a boy.

"Luckily garbage isn't my line. And luckily I don't take orders from you. Nor from any Vincent. Not anymore."

"Damn you, Cagan. You never did know your place."

"It's good to see you, too, Beaumont. Missed you at the high-school reunion."

"She's my fiancée!"

A silence fell between the two men, a silence pregnant with bitter memories. Garret's gaze remained cool and mocking. "So she is." Garret smiled. "Lucky lady."

"She never wanted you!"

Garret laughed softly. "No! So you think a woman like Noelle really prefers you, a guy who keeps his pompous bottom glued to the seat of his chair behind a desk in his daddy's bank, counting his daddy's money? Do you think she'd even look at you if it weren't for your daddy's money, Vincent?"

Beaumont's pale face went even paler. "Why you bast— I want you off this case."

"That's too bad because I just put myself in charge." Garret's white teeth gleamed, and his bold dark eyes laughed at the other man. He turned to the patrolman. "Johnson, I thought I ordered the street cleared."

Two officers grabbed Beaumont whose high-pitched nasal yelps of rage followed Garret. "Cagan, you always were white trash."

Garret's mouth thinned. He'd cut his teeth on that particular insult. The image of his beautiful, vital Noelle being tied to that white-faced wimp for the rest of her life nauseated Garret.

Beaumont's thin features were reflected in the window of the antique shop. Garret jammed the butt of his shotgun viciously into the reflection, shattering the glass, then climbed inside, mindless of the last falling shards that sprinkled down on the back of his leather jacket.

The bottom floor of the elegant shop was empty. Garret threaded his way silently through the darkened aisles of opulent French salon furniture, pastries of gilt, whims in marble, and tapestries, all laid out as though they were items in a supermarket. Every object in the shop was special, rare, one-of-a-kind, like the woman who had carefully selected them.

The gun had been fired from the top floor. Garret decided to look for Noelle there. He raced past the elevator, taking the stairs instead. When he reached the top floor, he threw himself against the wall, panting to catch his breath. His cheek felt hot and sweaty against the cool bricks as he waited, listening to the silence.

Suddenly he kicked the door of the stairwell open, then jumped aside and took cover behind the wall again while the metal door clanged noisily.

Nothing. Not a sound other than echoes of the door. Not a single bullet blasting the open doorway.

He was right.

Damn her. Only Noelle...

"Noelle!"

No answer.

"It's me, Garret. I'm coming in. Don't do anything crazy...." That was asking the impossible.

The wooden floor creaked as he moved across it.

"Go away!" Her voice came out of the darkness. It was hushed and faint with what sounded like fright. "He'll kill me."

Garret laughed low in his throat. She never gave up, even when she knew she was cornered.

"The hell he will, you little liar! I'll kill you myself for pulling a stunt like this!"

Garret rushed inside. He pulled the door closed, started to go after her, then hesitated, remembering all he had was ten minutes. Maybe not that much. The guys down there were jumpy, ready for action, just as he'd been.

He turned, locked the door, crouching all the time, keeping his body hidden in the tangled confusion of ancient brass beds, gilt mirrors and porcelains.

He heard a panicked scuffle at the other end of the shop and raced for it. When he reached the far corner of the room, there was no one there.

A gun glinted from a table beside a set of antique Venetian wineglasses. There was a black duffel bag, half-open, with loose green bills spilling out of it. He grabbed the bag, accidentally smashing a glass.

A gasp of horror came from above him.

He looked up and saw slender shapely legs encased in dark hose disappearing up the ladder into the darkness. He caught a glimpse of sexy black lace underwear.

He threw his shotgun and the bag to the floor and sprang across the shop, up the ladder with the quick grace of an Indian and grabbed her by the ankle.

A black high-heeled shoe came off and struck him above the eye.

"Ouch!" he growled. "Damn you!"

She kicked wildly. Her other heel nicked him in the forehead. The blow made him madder at her than he'd ever been. Blood trickled down the side of his face.

He merely tightened his grip on her ankle. "Noelle, you're kicking my face to pulp!" More softly, he added, "*Chère*, I know he's gone! I know you deliberately let him get away! I came in here to help you get out of this scrape." She tried to scramble free and accidentally kicked his cheek again, but despite the pain his grip remained iron hard. "I'll book you if you kick me again."

She kicked even harder

"Dammit! I swear I will." He pulled at her foot, and she almost lost her hold. "I'm not going to let go. I'm as stubborn as you, you hellcat brat. Are you coming down the ladder, or do I have to drag you down it?" He yanked hard on her ankle again, and she screamed.

The moment she stopped fighting him, he felt it.

She stilled. There was a tense silence as she clung to the ladder sulkily. He held on to her ankle while they both struggled to catch their breath.

He looked up and then away, but not before he registered the shape of flawless long legs and black lace beneath her flowing gray wool dress.

"Okay, Garret," she whispered. "You win—like always."

He backed warily down the ladder, not sure she would come after him. But she did.

"I don't always win, *chère*." His deep voice was as bitterly angry as hers. "I remember one night when I lost everything I ever thought I wanted...you...our baby..."

She went white.

His hands circled her waist possessively and he pulled her down in such a way that he made her body slide suggestively against the length of his. "*Chère* . . ."

She jumped back as if his touch was fire. "You promised my father you wouldn't bother me, ever again."

"Easy." Through the wool his hands could feel the subtle voluptuous warmth of her flesh. "I came here to save you, *chère*."

When her feet touched the floor, he kept holding her closely, his fingers digging through the soft charcoal wool of her elegant dress.

"Well, you can take your hands off me now," she commanded haughtily, although she did not lift her eyes to meet his.

Once he had been her servant. Hers to command in such an arrogant way. The yard boy who was dark from the sun, who got sweaty from hard physical work she and the rest of her family were too good to do.

No more.

Vaguely he was aware of her lowered lashes trembling against her flushed cheeks, of the slight tremor in her hands that pushed against him.

So—she wanted him still. Despite everything that had happened. But she was ashamed of those feelings. Just as she'd been ashamed when she'd been a young girl hiding herself behind the lace curtain of her upstairs window, watching him, the cook's son, as he'd toiled in the broiling Louisiana afternoon heat. Just as she'd been ashamed two years ago that it was his child she was carrying.

Noelle thought he was not good enough to want. She was going to marry Beaumont. Garret knew all about rich people and what they thought valuable—social connections, status.

"You damn little..." Instead of obeying her, he pulled her against his body until every muscular inch was pressed into the softness of hers.

Dammit. He didn't want her to feel so good.

"I'll let you go," he whispered, "but only if you promise not to run from me, *chère*. It seems like all your life you've been running...from me."

Spirals of flame-red curls spilled down her back and tangled in his fingers like skeins of flowing silk.

"For good cause."

The old anger rippled through him, but he held her so tightly he could not help being aware of her as a woman. As always just her nearness drove him crazy. Her stylish gray cashmere dress clung to her curves, outlining the shape of her breasts, the slender turn of her hips, leaving very little to his imagination. Vaguely he was aware of a subtle fragrance—her perfume enveloping him. It was sensual, barely tamed—like the woman. Once, when they'd been in bed, she had told him the scent was made of the *Moschata*, musk rose, a flower that grew wild on the Mediterranean coast. It was a rare, expensive scent—like the woman.

"Look at me, Noelle."

She twisted her face away from his.

"I said look at me."

Her long-lashed eyes lifted slowly. They were tawny, dark golden orbs, bright with dread and some other unnameable emotion as she stared searchingly up at his harsh features.

She began to tremble in earnest then.

It was nearly two years since he'd last seen her, two years since he'd last held her. Two years since that terrible night when she'd nearly died. Two years since she'd run away to Australia and stayed there.

Her family had been scandalized and made her go.

Because of him.

He'd told himself it was over, that he wanted her gone.

How wrong he'd been. He stared at her. Her face was even more exquisite than he remembered. She was half Creole. Her skin was pale, translucent; her hair wild red tangles; her mouth, full and parted. Her brows and lashes jet black.

He felt the full force of her beauty, and then the surge of his old hunger. He still wanted her. As much as he had when he'd been a kid, when he'd been in awe of her money and her daddy's power.

He wanted to hold her, to taste her, to take her to bed and stay there for days. Even though he despised her. Even though he despised himself for still feeling anything for her.

She was beautiful. Yes, no matter how much trouble she was, she was lovely—a tantalizing masterpiece of female flesh designed especially to drive him crazy. No other woman would ever seem as beautiful, at least not to him. But she would never think he was good enough.

That was a laugh.

"Damn you, Noelle. You taught me to love." He bit the side of his mouth till he tasted blood. "And to hate."

"Damn you, Garret. You taught me things...I wish I could forget, too." But her voice was a choked whisper as his had been, dying away in the silence of the darkened shop. There was a look in her eyes that made him wonder what she might be feeling.

He moved so that the light from the window fell across his virile features, and she saw his face.

"I hurt you," she said softly. At the sight of his bruised cheek and cut forehead, her expression became one of tender remorse. "I didn't mean to."

She reached up to brush the blood from his brow, but he jumped back, startled by her tenderness, suddenly as afraid of her touch as she was of his.

"Garret, I was just . . ."

He eyed her warily, then let her go, almost pushing her away. The gentleness in her gaze pierced all the way to his soul. The thing he trusted least from her was kindness. "I'll do it myself."

He wiped the blood out of his eyes with the back of his wrist. Then he glanced out the window. In the street the police were massing to storm the shop. He was running out of time.

Garret turned back to Noelle. "So tell me what you were doing up here all alone shooting down at me and my friends."

"I—I—"

"Tell me," he ordered.

When she was silent he wiped an arm across a table stacked with priceless ruby-red Venetian crystal, and swept two dozen glasses to the floor.

"No!"

"Tell me!"

She stared at the glimmering scarlet bits of glass. "Garret, those glasses cost thousands of dollars."

"Do you think I give a damn?"

He picked up his shotgun and swept another table free of glasses.

"Garret! I—I . . . I wasn't shooting at anybody!"

He headed for a tall bird.

"Not the majolica crane *jardinière*!" she screamed, lunging at him before he could smash it.

"The what?" He cocked a quizzical dark brow. Then he grabbed her, seizing her wrists in a grip that hurt, crushing her breasts into the metal zipper of his leather jacket.

"That's all you care about, isn't it? Glass birds! Things! Money! You're just like the rest of your family."

"Garret, don't break it. I'll tell you everything."

He could hear the cops in the building downstairs.

"You better make it quick." His voice was low, but dangerous nevertheless.

"It all happened so fast. I wasn't thinking clearly."

"You never do."

"In the bank I saw he was just a kid. A poor desperate boy. H-he seemed so alone. Like Louis somehow."

"Leave Louis out of this!"

A wild, lost look was in her eyes. She struggled to continue. "He was bungling everything. When he was going out of the door, I grabbed the money and ran. I thought if I took it and returned it to the bank, he wouldn't be in so much trouble. I thought he'd run away, but he followed me here. The bank foreclosed on his mother's house. His mother's very sick. She needs an operation—"

"And you believed him?"

"I told him if he'd leave the money and go, I'd stay here alone for a while and give him time to get away. I said he could come back in a few days. I promised to help him."

"You what?"

She swallowed convulsively. "I—"

"Never mind! Listen to me, you little fool. Those were cops you were shooting at."

"I wasn't shooting at them! I shot way over their heads."

"They don't know that! What matters is that you helped a bank robber escape. You must do exactly as I say. When the other cops get here, let me do the talking. I'll tell them there was a struggle. The robber got away. You were so scared you were afraid to come out—"

"But..."

He gave her a derisive look. "For once in your life, keep your mouth shut."

A tense silence enveloped them. He picked up the gun and wiped it free of fingerprints. They both listened to the galloping footsteps ascending the stairs.

He realized the enormity of what he was doing.

"Garret . . . Why are you doing this for me?"

He turned toward her. His eyes slid downward from her beautiful face, over her body as if he couldn't help himself. Unwanted memories of all that she'd been to him assailed him.

He said nothing for a long moment. He just studied the beauty of lush breasts pushing sexily against gray wool, her narrow waist, the curve of her slender hips. Not by so much as the flicker of an eyelid did he reveal that the mere sight of her body made him ache like a raw boy with a feverish hunger.

"Because."

Words alone couldn't convey his reason.

He looked at her. Something in his eyes must have betrayed him because she glanced wildly away.

He swaggered toward her like a menacing giant in the darkness, cornering her against a table. She gave a little cry of fright and tried to spring past him. He slid his arms around her, crushing her with his masculine power until she screamed.

"Shut up, *chère*," he whispered, pressing his body into hers so hard that the table ground into her hips.

"Garret, I don't want you. Not anymore."

"No?" He laughed softly. One brown hand fingered the silky tendrils that fell against her cheek. "So you're going to marry Beau . . . and not Raoul."

"I never wanted Raoul. He was..." She stopped herself.

"Well, Beau's a better choice for a woman like you. He's a man who can assure your position in the world. A man who'll sire babies you'll want...instead of babies you don't want...."

Tears welled in her golden eyes.

"Congratulations, *chère*. And since I'm not on the social register and won't be invited to the wedding, you won't mind if I take my kiss from the bride now."

She began to struggle as if she did mind, but Garret's mouth fastened on hers quickly, savagely, devouring her full soft lips with a greedy passion.

She opened her mouth. The tips of their tongues touched. Hotly. Wetly.

Her response was as swift and as fierce as his. He felt her trembling. Her skin was velvet fire. Her fingertips buried themselves in his thick black hair. She was arching her body into his. He felt her nails digging into his scalp. He forgot his hate and was engulfed by passion. The world was spinning.

The touch of her, the taste of her sweet, hot flesh made him whole.

It didn't matter what she had done to him. Or to Louis. Even the baby that had died no longer mattered.

Garret could have kissed her endlessly.

Instead he shoved her away, jarring the table so that a porcelain vase fell and smashed.

He caught a quick shallow breath.

"Let's just say," he began in a grim cynical tone, "that I'm doing this for old time's sake."

He noted the quick flash of pain in her eyes.

"You owe me nothing. Do you understand me? Nothing. No matter what happens, stay away from me, *chère*. Stay away from Louis. And I'll stay away from you."

There was a frantic banging at the door before it crashed open.

Then the herd of police was upon them.

Two

In the darkening afternoon the Mercedes raced along the forest road. Inside the car the red-haired woman with the haunted, brandy-colored eyes wore cream-white silk and gold jewelry. Her nails were long and polished, her skin as soft as satin, and her makeup lush and perfect.

Noelle felt hurried, upset. Usually the drive to Garret's home and Martin House took less than an hour from New Orleans. Today there had been a wreck on the causeway, and she'd been driving for over two hours.

The *Times-Picayune* lay open on top of Garret's leather jacket on the passenger seat. There was a picture of Noelle wrapped in Garret's jacket. Another picture of Garret. The headline read, Detective Garret Cagan Suspended Pending Investigation into Bank Robbery.

Garret had disobeyed orders to save her. He had lied to protect her, jeopardized everything he had worked so hard to attain. Now he was blamed because the bank robber had escaped. Beaumont and her own father were doing everything they could to have Garret thrown off the force for incompetency.

Two years ago she'd lost her baby and lain in a New Orleans hospital dying. She'd wanted to die. Her family had blamed Garret, and when she had finally recovered they had made her see how terrible he was. She had promised herself, promised her family, that never again would she have anything to do with Garret Cagan. But he was in trouble, and it was all her fault. Her own family was making things worse for him. She felt a sharp prickle of guilt. So many times—*too* many times—Garret had suffered that fate.

In her plush steel cocoon Noelle was physically insulated from the rich odor of the bayou, from the poverty of the rickety clapboard houses and dilapidated docks she passed. But not emotionally insulated. The bewildering mosaic of winding waterways, the blind lakes, even the houses brought old memories vividly back to life. For this was where she and Garret had grown up—she in beautiful Martin House and Garret in a humble three-room shack on a few scrap acres behind her father's plantation. This was the land she loved more than any other—with its twisting bayous and semitropical swamps. When she was six her grandmother had become alarmed that Noelle was growing up too wild in the country. *Grand-mère* had insisted on moving into New Orleans so that Noelle could be tamed by city life. From then on the family had only used Martin House on holidays, weekends and the summers.

Noelle had not been to Martin House since her return to Louisiana. She dreaded the thought of seeing Garret, and she knew she was the last person he would want to see. But she had no choice. She tried to tell herself that he could no longer be a danger to her. Not now. Not since she was at last leading the conventional life her family had always wished her to lead.

She'd had two years to forget him. Two years of adventure and hardship in a hostile land. Two years of homesickness in Australia. Two years to deal with the feelings of emptiness, pain, guilt and bitter regret—and all because of him.

At last because of *Grand-mère*'s declining health, Noelle had returned to Louisiana. But not to come back to Garret. She had decided to live the life *Grand-mère* had dreamed of her living. Noelle had become a buyer for Mama's antique shop. She wore silk dresses to work, attended the right parties, dated the right men; men with impeccable social pedigrees to satisfy *Grand-mère*, men with vast wealth and power to please Papa. There were stories about her social successes in the society columns, rumors that she would marry Beau, her "childhood sweetheart." Her family thought she was happy and settled at last. *Grand-mère* would take her hand and hold it in her frail shaking fingers, and Noelle would know that at last *Grand-mère* was proud of her. But sometimes at night, when Noelle couldn't sleep, she would stare out her window at the sultry moon neslted low in the pines. She would feel wild with the old gnawing restlessness. And she would remember the one forbidden man who had dispelled it.

Only scandalous Mama had noticed. "Something wrong, *chère*? You feel better if you tell your mama," Bibi had said.

Beautiful, wild Mama. Mama with hair even brighter than her own. Mama, who'd been born in a tar-paper shack in the Deep Delta lowlands of Louisiana and scratched her way to the top. Mama who'd had three husbands, each of them richer than the one before. Mama, the Hollywood actress who'd had an affair with Papa when he was a senator and destroyed his political career. Mama, who'd had to get pregnant before Papa dared go against his family and make her his second wife. Mama who was still as incorrigible as ever.

When Noelle would turn away, Mama would pet her hair. "It's that Detective Cagan, isn't it, *chère*? You can't forget him. They don't understand, *Grand-mère* and Papa. You're like me. You have my passion. You have to follow your own path, *chère*."

"You're the only one who does not despise me for my weak character."

"Weak character!" Mama had laughed lightly at that. "*Chère*, I do not consider it weak, no. If anything the experience of love only strengthens a woman's character."

Noelle tried not to listen to her mother. She had never wanted to be like Mama. But this afternoon, Noelle had run away and was secretly defying *Grand-mère* and Papa.

It felt strange driving down this road again. Strange and terrifying to think of seeing Cagan.

He'd been so fierce in the shop. But passionate, too. He hated her for what she'd done to him. Just as she sometimes hated him. But she'd seen the hunger in his eyes every time he looked at her. And then he'd kissed her. Maybe the big bad cop hadn't forgiven her, but he wasn't as immune to her as he pretended he was.

Noelle Martin's bitten lips tasted salty; her slim fingers were clenched tightly on the steering wheel. She wanted a cigarette, but she had quit smoking. So she grabbed a tape and jammed it into her player. Instantly the Mercedes was flooded by Chopin's hauntingly lovely "Raindrop Prelude." Her favorite piece. Not that it soothed her. Her emotions were in such a state of turmoil about the prospect of facing Garret that nothing could have calmed her.

Even as her silvery blue sports car purred past the weird dead forest where moss had grown too thickly, smothering the cypress trees and converting them into figures of gauntness and dread, she whispered shakily to herself, "You could go home now—even now. It's not too late. No one would ever know you had this crazy impulse."

Home—back to the glitter and safety of New Orleans. Back to the Garden District. Back to her world of wealth and privilege and rank. Back to Beaumont, whom she would be married forever and ever to.

Dear God . . .

She needed something to drink, but her can of soda was empty.

Stubbornly she pressed down the accelerator pedal. She had to see Garret. Even if they'd all forbidden her to. Even though he himself had made it clear he never wanted to see her again.

He was in trouble because of her. Sometimes it seemed that his life and hers were woven so tightly together it was impossible to separate her soul from his. Garret's mother, Mannie, had been the kindly cook in the Martin household. Noelle had grown up adoring her. Noelle remembered that dark night Garret's father and little brother had died. She'd been six years old when it happened. Father and son had been walking home after fishing at the bayou. A truck full of logs had been rushing past them on a curve. One of the bands holding the logs to the truck bed had snapped, and the logs had broken free and crushed father and son. Noelle had convinced her father to hire Garret to help their gardener.

Garret had worked hard after school and every summer to help support his mother and sister. He'd been wild, but he'd worked his way through college and struggled through graduate school while he'd worked full-time on the police force. He'd risen unbelievably fast in his career. He and his mother had started a Cajun restaurant in New Orleans, Mannie's, that had become a phenomenal success. He'd married Annie, and they had torn down the shack he'd grown up in and built their darling cottage on his land behind Martin House. He kept a houseboat moored in a particularly beautiful bend of the bayou a couple of miles from his house, a place that had been a favorite childhood haunt of his. He had a yacht in New Orleans docked near Mannie's and he slept on it sometimes. But there had been a time when Garret had become so desperate, he'd almost thrown it all away. Because of her, to win her respect—he'd done it all.

Sometimes it seemed that all her life *Grand-mère* and Papa had forbidden her to do the things that had really mattered to her. They'd been against Garret. She had wanted to be a nurse; they had stopped her. *Grand-mère* had been horrified at the thought of a Martin being employed in a hospital working as a mere nurse.

Grand-mère was of the old school. "Girls in your position marry well. If marriage and children are not enough, you can serve the community in dozens of acceptable ways. There are boards ladies can serve on, volunteer work, charities..."

As a child Noelle had collected injured and stray animals. That had never been "acceptable," either, although in the end, *Grand-mère* had had a special little cottage built in the backyard to house Noelle's menagerie.

"Your soft heart will be your doom," *Grand-mère* had predicted direly on more than one occasion, but she had softened her prediction with one of her rare smiles.

Now, after her stroke, *Grand-mère* smiled even less than before. For a while she had been unable to talk. Tottering around on her silver cane, she was no longer the formidable matriarch. She seemed unbelievably delicate, but she was dearer to Noelle than ever. Noelle didn't ever want to hurt her again.

Noelle gripped the steering wheel. Garret had lied about the bank robber and thereby jeopardized a job he valued immensely because of her. Why?

The wet road that led to Garret's house was a shiny black ribbon curving relentlessly beneath a tunnel of deep green velvet. Her family's plantation and Martin House lay just beyond his land. And beyond Martin House was Sweet Seclusion, a crumbling plantation house attached to several thousand acres of sugarcane land, all owned by Raoul Girouard, a tough, remote man much older than herself, to whom scandal and romance and mystery had attached itself. There was not a mother in the parish who did not tremble if their daughters even glanced at the dangerously attractive Raoul. *Grand-mère* disliked all the Girouards intensely. So did Garret. For a while Raoul had fancied Noelle's baby sister, Eva. Noelle had been the cause of their breaking up.

At the moment, though, Noelle wasn't thinking about Raoul, or the problems he had caused her. Her thoughts were focused on Garret.

During happier times, Garret had told her that the live-oak alley that led to his house had been planted over a hundred years ago by a prosperous sugarcane planter, an ancestor of his, that once there had been the glimmer of white columns at its end, but that the plantation house had burned during the Civil War. Before falling on hard times themselves, the Girouards had either bought or stolen the Cagan family land acre by acre.

The shack Garret had grown up in had been torn down. Now there was only Garret's modern cottage, built on brick pilings, Louisiana style, on the original site of the plantation house. Behind his cottage lay the smooth green sheet of the bayou.

She passed a marsh-ringed lagoon where a fishing boat was docked. Ramshackle buildings, trailers and automobiles sat in the backwash.

Noelle Martin saw No Trespassing signs in the high grasses along the bayou's edges. Other signs were nailed crookedly to tree trunks in the dense forest. The signs had not been there two years ago, and they made her journey seem more forbidding. Garret didn't want trespassers. He didn't want her.

She rounded a curve. Suddenly a lone mailbox loomed out of the high weeds beside the road. She braked and read the name, Garret Cagan, painted on it in neat, bold black letters. The name, Louis Cagan, was scribbled in a child's illegible hand beneath his father's. Louis had clumsily painted a red crawfish beside his name. The father's name had been repainted recently, but the son's had not. That made Noelle wonder if Louis had been banished again to live in exile with his grandmother in her nearby cottage.

Noelle remembered Louis—big soft eyes, golden hair— a thin, delicately-built, sensitive boy, who was nothing like his father. He had an incredible imagination and knew the swamp like the back of his hand. Louis had been four when she'd last seen him and still scarred from having witnessed his mother's death. The first words he'd spoken since Annie's death had been to Noelle. "Don't leave!" he'd cried, hurling himself into her arms when she'd told him goodbye. She'd hugged him close, her tears mingling with his.

She'd carried him in her heart, his loss as vivid and heartbreaking as the loss of her own child. What had happened to that dear lonely little boy in the two years since she'd seen him?

The sun vanished behind a black cloud, and darkness crept over the forest. A cool wind had begun to blow from the north, and she remembered a cold front was due. Her stomach knotted, and she sucked in a deep breath. She felt so strange, so scared, but she'd come this far.

The private driveway to Garret's cottage was a short, oyster-shell zigzag through trees hung with verdant creepers and wisteria. She drove slowly, but all too soon his unpainted cypress house with brick trim and green shutters came into view.

The house seemed lost and forlorn looking in the shadowy gloom.

"Mon Dieu…" She stared at it wordlessly, trying not to remember, and yet remembering everything. As a child she'd often come here seeking Garret, so he would take her fishing in the bayou. As an adolescent, she'd come by to tempt him. When she'd gotten older, he'd brought her here and made love to her.

Because of her family they'd parted. She'd been seventeen when they'd sent her away to school. He'd married. He'd built a house here. Louis had been born. Then an excon who was trying to kill Garret had shot Annie by mistake. Garret had blamed himself. Two years later, Noelle had tried to comfort him in his grief. They'd had an affair again. Briefly. Before the scandal, before her family had sent her away because of him a second time.

Noelle shook herself. Today there was only silence. Only the trees, tense and close.

It was just a house, a house in the woods, she told herself frantically, but there was a buzzing in her head that wouldn't stop. And her throat was tightening.

Just a house… Just a quaintly charming house of Louisiana colonial design, a cypress cottage nestled under the gnarled branches of a live oak, where once a happy family had lived. Just a house that was neatly maintained by the grim man who now lived in it alone.

The blood drained from her face.

Garret's house could never be just a house to her. This place was a part of her. As he was.

Every window was immaculately shined. The iron work and shutters were painted. Garret's garden was planted in straight rows of emerald green. He'd never been one to shirk physical work. Garret's airboat was tied at the dock. His fishing nets were hung on a fence to dry. She felt his methodical organized presence seeping into her bones.

Everything was just as it was.

No...

Once Louis's toys had been strewn around. His bike. Carlotta, the basset hound Noelle had given him, had been lazing on the porch. Tiger, Louis's striped gray cat with the green eyes, had been howling about something.

The house seemed too still, too perfect. Like a dead person laid out for a wake. Like something that had once been alive but no longer was.

Like Garret who had buried himself alive.

She cut the engine, and Chopin's climactic finale died abruptly. She grabbed Garret's jacket and opened the door. The cool muggy air pierced her with that peculiar marsh smell of damp and decay. The last of the late-afternoon light was going, and the dense forest was filled with an eerie silence. It was getting colder, and she'd forgotten to bring a coat.

Although Garret's white truck was parked in front of the house, no light shone from the windows, and his pirogue was gone. Noelle remembered that he liked to hunt and trap on winter weekends. Sometimes he fished to help supply the restaurant. With Annie dead and Louis living with Annie's mother, there was no telling when Garret was coming home.

He would be back, though, and she wasn't leaving until she saw him.

The cream-white folds of Noelle's thin silk dress swished as she forced herself to walk toward the house. His leather jacket was slung over her arm. Her heels made hollow sounds like faltering heartbeats as she climbed the stairs and walked across the porch. She began to knock. When he didn't answer, she sagged, shivering, against the wall. Slowly as she stood there, her surroundings came to life, the humming, buzzing, droning, splashing cacophony of the bayou. The sun was going down in a blaze of scarlet through the trees.

There was a mysterious beauty about the forest, but the loneliness of the place made her ache for Garret. How had he gone on living out here? By himself? Rejecting Louis?

A thin whine mounted steadily. Something bit her on the ankle, then the other leg. First there was one mosquito, then a few more, then millions, ravenous after a day of fasting in grassy marshlands. She kept slapping her legs until they were red and stinging with pain; until the cold, wet air was alive with them and there were too many of them biting her to slap them all.

She was jumping, hopping, shivering from the cold. If she didn't go inside, she would either freeze to death or be eaten alive.

Her fingers trembled on the latch of the screen door.

Garret would be furious. He wouldn't want her inside the house.

Mosquitoes bit Noelle on the nose, her eyelids.

It was wrong to go in with him gone.

A sharp icy blast of wet air swept the porch. Lightning flashed from the bottom of a low-bellied cloud, and cold rain began to gust in torrents.

She pulled the screen door open and ran inside.

The single lantern in the bow of the pirogue glowed eerily through the floating wisps of ground fog. It was two o'clock in the morning, and Garret Cagan was bone weary. Suddenly a bolt of lightning scribbled exquisite patterns across the wet ink-black sky. The norther was violent and dangerous, but beautiful. For a microsecond the marsh was illuminated, and the gaunt arms of dead cypress trees cloaked with moss were silhouetted against the brilliance. Then the blackness was blacker than before, the stillness, stiller.

The bow of Garret's pirogue was piled high with nutria pelts. The grasses and traps had been alive with animals. In a bucket, the dozen crabs he'd caught made scratching sounds. A stringer full of fish was tied onto the stern. It had been a good afternoon and night for checking his traps and fishing.

But it was getting colder, and despite his jacket, Garret was freezing. It had rained off and on all evening. He ached with exhaustion from the long hours sloshing alongside his pirogue or poling it. He was starving, too, and sick of the mosquitoes. He wanted to get home, light the stove, make a pot of gumbo with his catch.

A violent tremor seized Garret, and he bent over the pole of his pirogue, pushing the shallow dugout craft along the canal with the skill of a Cajun born to the bayou. Before Annie's death, Garret had hated these cold, wet winter nights. He'd preferred staying home with her and little Louis in the cozy warmth of their cottage.

Now he almost never stayed home. When he got in from work—he'd been putting in hellish hours at the restaurant ever since he'd been suspended from the force—he either took the truck and went to see Louis, who now lived at Annie's mother's, or he took the pirogue out into the swamp.

An hour later, when Garret's pirogue glided up to his dock, a blue-gray fog was rising from the blind lake. He'd put out his lantern, but every time he moved the pole, the water glittered with the silent fire of phosphorescent plankton. Cajuns called it ghost fire. Garret's pole clattered against the wooden dock. A flock of ducks exploded from its feeding grounds and sprayed the night with a shower of falling pixie dust.

Garret stared in wonder. He had never seen the ghost fire so bright before. It meant good luck.

His handsome mouth twisted bitterly.

Good luck.

Not for him.

He'd never been lucky.

He'd been poor but ambitious. He'd seen enough of the rich life to want it and feel shut out. He'd lost everything he'd fought so hard for—Annie, Louis, Noelle. And now his job.

He grabbed his ten-gauge, slung the nutria pelts over his shoulder and strode toward his cottage. He'd loved two women. The one he'd wanted the most thought she was too good for him. The one he'd married had died. Garret still felt guilt over that because the crook who had shot her had been gunning for him.

Annie could have raised Louis; Garret didn't know how. What did a man like him know about raising a kid like Louis? Louis seemed so fragile, so like Annie. Garret was afraid to try, afraid he'd do it all wrong. Still, every time he thought of Louis, he felt a tug of remorse. It was his own fault Louis wouldn't talk.

When Garret had become a cop, he'd known that he was risking his life every day he worked, but his own life had always seemed a cheap thing to him. He'd never thought of the risk to Annie and Louis. Because of his own selfish blindness, Louis was growing up a lonely, silent, mother-less boy. He was fatherless, too. And Garret couldn't forgive himself.

Annie had died because of him, and he was forgetting her. He wasn't doing right by her child. He never longed for her anymore. Without a photograph he couldn't picture her face. Their time together now seemed so far away. He felt so cold, so hard—almost inhuman sometimes.

It was Noelle he remembered. Noelle, whom he'd grown up with. Noelle, the rich, spoiled glitter girl he had always wanted. Noelle, who had betrayed him twice. Noelle, who'd destroyed Louis all over again.

Why the hell had he put the only thing he still had left, his career, on the line for her?

Three

The minute he stepped inside his house, Garret's sixth sense told him something was different. He hadn't seen the blue sports car hidden by the trees. His black gaze scanned the kitchen, den and dining room but found nothing amiss.

There was a half-empty soda can in the sink. His leather jacket was on the table, but he didn't see it. His mouth twisted in wry self-deprecation. Must be his tiredness making his cop paranoia work overtime. One of the reasons he went out into the swamp alone was to get that sort of junk out of his mind.

Hell, there was no one here. It wasn't as if he had friends anymore.

He propped his ten-gauge in a corner and set a pot of water on the stove for the crabs. He opened a cabinet and pulled out his bottle of whiskey and took a swig straight from the bottle. After a while he took another pull from the bottle, then a few more. The liquor burned his throat, but it warmed him all the way down. It took the edge off his loneliness; it removed the swamp damp and chill out of his bones. He shrugged out of his jacket.

He shouldn't drink alone. Not straight out of the bottle. Hell. He did a lot of things he shouldn't do. Still, the next time he felt the need, he splashed his whiskey into a glass.

Swiftly, skillfully he cleaned the fish, wrapped all but two in butcher paper and put them in the freezer. When he was done, he turned off the stove. Tomorrow he'd cook the crabs.

Then he saw the mud on the floor. Damn. Later for that, too. Wearily he pulled off his thick-soled rubber boots and took them out to the porch. He stalked across the room to the bedroom. The thick carpet in the bedroom absorbed the thud of his heavy tread as he crossed the bedroom and went into the bathroom. He peeled off the rest of his wet clothes and quickly took a hot shower.

Vapors were still steaming off his bronzed skin when he opened the bedroom door and stepped into the pitch-black room. The whiskey and the hot water had relaxed him.

A soft sound came from the bed.

Something white flashed in the darkness.

A shiver of apprehension traced the length of his spine. He wasn't alone, and he was as naked as the day he was born. His shotgun was in the other room.

His every predatory instinct sprang instantly to life. Panic and long-conditioned reflexes made him lunge toward the bed to grab the intruder. Garret was intent upon immobilizing whomever had broken into his cabin and was laying in wait for him.

His muscled legs straddled a slim body on the bed. His callused hand ran the delicate length of a slender throat, touched the delicious softness of a breast.

A woman.

In shock he jerked his hand away just as she started to scream. His other hand, which had been tangled in long strands of her silken hair, now clamped over her mouth. She squirmed, twisting her neck, flailing her arms, writhing, and he heard the sound of silk shredding. She bit him, and this time, it was he who screamed.

He cursed in low but vivid French.

She began to struggle in earnest. More silk tore. He only pushed her deeper into the bed, using the weight of his more powerful body to crush out her resistance. He felt her breasts pushing against his chest. Her heart was pounding. She was gasping for air. Her strength was nothing to his, and he subdued her effortlessly.

He inhaled the haunting sweetness of musk rose—a woman's perfume. Something about that scent was oddly, disquietingly familiar. But because of the whiskey, he couldn't think clearly.

Her body was twisting against his, rubbing itself tightly against his naked muscles. Since he didn't have a stitch on, her every movement of silk and skin made him intimately aware of her.

Damn.

She tried to kick him, but the soft sensation of her leg against his naked flesh only rocked his senses. He willed himself not to react to the feminine feel of her body beneath his, but he was aware of piercingly hot sensations of pleasure every time her legs brushed against his thighs. He cursed himself roundly again. He hadn't had a woman under him in more than a year, especially not one as soft and as delicate as this one.

Her nearness, her constant wiggling made him start to tremble. "Stop moving," he rasped. "I won't hurt you."

But she kept moving, and he felt an aftershock of male desire every time her legs or hands brushed him.

The feel of her, the heat of her—she was slim but lushly built—the smell of her, were all faintly familiar, and aroused in him feelings of confused mutiny. He was shaking with a starving need for the woman and was furious at her and at himself because of his reaction.

"If you didn't want this, you shouldn't have climbed into my bed in the middle of the night, *chère*," he whispered in a low sardonic drawl slurred by whiskey and angry desire. "Stop moving before I do something we both regret."

"Garret..." A woman's voice, breathless and faint with fear, slightly accented, as soft as velvet, filled the darkness with its voluptuous femininity.

Instant recognition went through him. Noelle... The musk rose... Subconsciously he must have known at once. That was why his body had reacted.

Knowing it was her made him hotter than ever. She had climbed into his bed in the middle of the night. That could only mean one thing—she was inviting him to bed her.

His heart filled with dark hate. He stiffened. The last time she'd come to him, and he'd given in to his desire for her, she'd nearly destroyed him.

The warmth of her breath wafted over his dark face. He remembered their kiss in her shop. It was a struggle to maintain his sanity and not to take her instantly, swiftly.

"Noelle? What are...?"

"I—I was waiting for you," she murmured. "I came out to see you, but you weren't here. I came inside because of the mosquitoes and the rain. Then you didn't come back, and I got so tired. I must have fallen asleep...hours ago. I didn't know who you were at first."

"You shouldn't have come," he said roughly, but he felt the old unwanted wildness she had always aroused building inside him.

Somewhere in the back of his mind a voice was shouting for him to run from the room, to leave her, to go before it was too late. He had vowed never again to give her the chance to ensnare his heart. But he felt dizzy, bewildered. The whiskey... Her nearness... His naked oak-hard thighs straddling her hips. Her body under his had always been a perfect fit.

"I want to go to the captain and tell him—"

"Stay the hell away from him! Do you hear me?"

She was the reincarnation of a thousand male fantasies. She was sweetness, femininity—a woman. She was the love of his youth. The fantasy girl who lived in a dreamworld just out of reach. The woman he had always wanted—no matter what she'd done. She had come back into his life after Annie's death when he was losing his mind to grief. Noelle had given herself to him, given him the will to go on living despite the tragedy. Her love and friendship, though casually given, had made Louis blossom, if ever so briefly.

Every male cell in Garret's body was on fire.

He released her and started to draw back.

Then she touched him.

As he had not been touched since she'd left him. As he'd dreamed of her touching him. With fingertips that were as hot as flame, as gentle as satin rippling down the hard length of his backbone.

"I want to hate you, too, Garret," she whispered with tears in her voice.

He wanted to resist her, but a blackness swam in front of his eyes. A madness gripped his heart. He was aware only of the velvet warmth of her fingertips gliding across his skin, touching him everywhere. He felt the damp and coolness of the November night. He saw the flashes of lightning and heard the intermittent crackle of thunder.

Her hands explored him gently. She was devouring his stubborn will by degrees, slowly, steadily wearing him down. And suddenly he was all mixed up. There was a throbbing ache in his gut. Her soft caresses were a wordless comfort in the darkness of his torment. He wanted to take her into his arms, to hold on to her, to stop being the hardened cop who had to act like he was too tough to feel anything. For two years he had ached for human touching, for her comfort. Suddenly he was shaking.

Her gentle hands touched his bare, muscled shoulders, slid around his neck, caressed his throat. It felt so good to be tenderly petted. Treacherously good. Somehow it eased the terrible anger inside him, so he didn't stop her. Her touch was tender and kind. Although he knew not to trust kindness from her, it was the one thing he longed for.

Once he had thought she was kind—and gentle, so different from him.

She turned her hand over and with the backs of her fingers she traced his brow, the length of his straight nose. Tenderly she stroked his cheek, the hard line of his jaw, taking inventory of his uncompromisingly masculine features like a blind person with her fingertips. He felt her hands in the curling blackness of his hair.

He'd been alone so long. He knew just how beautiful she was…and how treacherous. He imagined her coppery hair and her voluptuous, full-bosomed figure. Too well he remembered the flawless perfection of her features—her pale skin, her black winged brows, her startlingly whiskey-colored eyes fringed with thick sooty lashes, her aquiline nose, and her full, sensuous mouth.

He remembered her family as well, aristocrats, all of them, all but her scandalous mother anyway, people who thought their daughter too good to associate with a man who'd been their former cook's son, for a man who'd lived hard on the streets of New Orleans before he'd become a cop.

He swallowed to maintain control. Once he'd thought Noelle was different from her family. Now he knew better. Still, it would be so easy to take her, to use her, to forget, if only for one night.

The taste of whiskey was bitter and hot in his mouth. He wanted to replace the taste of it with the taste of Noelle.

If he did that, the senator would be gunning for him. He might never work as a cop in New Orleans again. He damn sure didn't want to spend the rest of his life cooking at Mannie's. But if he moved, he'd have to start over at the bottom in any other city police department—in the academy. If there was one thing Garret hated the thought of, it was being on the bottom again.

"Two years ago you all but destroyed me—for the second time. Not to mention what you did to Louis. What the hell are you doing here tonight?" Garret growled savagely.

Again her voice came, soft, throaty, filling the darkness like sexy French music. "You threw me out two years ago!"

"Because—"

"Because, like my family, you were too ready to believe the worst of me. I'm just as determined to forget you as you are to forget me. My family wants me to marry Beau. I wouldn't be here except last week you risked your job to save me despite what you thought I'd done to you."

"What I *thought*?" he snarled.

"Shh. I don't want to quarrel. Why can't we put the past behind us and just go on with our own lives? We grew up together. Can't we at least be friends? I came here because I want to help you get your job back. Then I saw that you're still out here all alone, and I can't bear the thought of that, of Louis growing up without even knowing you.

You can't shut the world out. No wonder Louis acts the way he does.''

"Forget Louis. Don't you go near him."

"Why?"

"I won't have him hurt all over again!"

"Oh, so you think he'll be okay if he hides from anything that might make him feel something?''

"Don't tell me how to live my life. Just go back to your world. You don't belong here. Not with me."

"I want to help you get out of this, Garret. Is that so wrong?''

"Yes," he muttered darkly. "Yes.... Go home. Where you belong.''

"Sometimes I wonder where I do belong."

His lips curved in cynical disbelief. "Well, you damn sure don't belong here. I know what you want. You don't give a damn about Louis or me." His tone was insolent. "And it's something your prim-and-proper Beaumont can't ever give you. You've always had a taste for the wrong kind of man.''

Once before he'd driven her away with words like that.

"No..." Her voice was raw with hurt.

He started to get up. He was halfway across the room when a series of low, heart-wrenching sobs stopped him. Noelle was crying. He had never been able to stand to hear a woman cry. Maybe the only reason she'd driven out here was to help him; maybe she really was worried about him. If that were true, he'd treated her like a brute. She sounded so utterly hopeless that his anger and determination melted.

He clenched his hands into fists. He had to go.

Another sob broke the silence.

She was crying because of him, and the sound of her unhappiness was unbearable. Every low sniffle and gasp tore at him.

He was stunned. Why couldn't he just walk out of the room and leave her? Why did she have this power over him?

He called to her across the darkness. "Noelle..."

He received no answer. Only more heartbreaking sobs.

Softly: "Don't cry, *chère*, no."

Still no answer. Nothing but darkness and the guilty knowledge that her misery was all his fault. He could see the shape of her. She lay on the bed, her face buried in his pillow, her flaming hair spilling over her slender body that was racked with sobs. She looked so tiny, so helpless—so utterly forlorn.

Because of him.

Some emotion that he didn't want and didn't understand pushed all else aside. He went to her and pulled her into his arms.

She felt hot and soft, all female. Skin to silk; man to woman. As always she felt incredibly good.

"Oh, Garret," she breathed. Her arms went around him. Her fingers threaded themselves through his hair. "You're so impossible, and yet I always get so mixed up when I'm around you. I want to hate you the same way you hate me. More than anything in the world, I want that. But I don't know what I feel. I only know I'm sorry that I've ruined everything for you again. And as for Louis—I loved him. I still do."

"Shut up about Louis!"

More sobs broke from her.

Garret's grip tightened around her. "There, there, Noelle. Shh, *chère*. I'm glad you're here," he murmured. "But you shouldn't have come." He stroked her back and her hair.

Finally she quieted and lay still against him. Slowly, once more, he grew aware of her body against his, of the light silken dress that lay between his skin and hers. She smelled of that wild Mediterranean flower, and he rubbed his hand across her cheek and tenderly kissed her forehead. He felt her lush breasts pressing against his bare chest; he felt her nipples bud into hardened tips. His breath caught in his throat.

"Noelle," he whispered warningly, "you should go."

She kissed his throat passionately. "Stay with me. If only for tonight. I know it's crazy, and I know tomorrow I'll hate myself more than ever. But...now...I just want to be with you."

He wanted to hate her, too, but the whiskey was blurring the hate, mixing it into a potent combination of desire and need and lonely desperation. He remembered the wild fear he'd felt in front of her shop when he'd been scared she might get gunned down the way Annie had. Very slowly he sank down beside her and pulled her against his body.

In the darkness, as he lay with her in his arms, he was too keenly aware of her warmth and softness to sleep. She kept him on edge, made him want to take her, but he was determined not to do that.

Some time during the night it began to rain, gently, sweetly, and she snuggled even closer to him.

She was a comfort, an unwanted one.

His first since he'd thrown her out two years ago.

Four

___

Noelle's dream was vivid, full color, truer than real life. She was alone in her mother's shop hiding behind a wild assortment of nineteenth-century statues and furniture: two immense stone lions from Russia, a carved-walnut bear love seat from the Black Forest, and a Biedermeier table.

She was alone with the gun and the stolen money. The cops were closing in on her.

They knew she'd helped the bank robber escape.

Only Garret wasn't there to save her. He had abandoned her as he had that other nightmarish night.

She was stumbling through a clutter of salon furniture, past an American staghorn chair trying to find the ladder that led to the attic and the roof. Only she could not find it.

The police kept coming closer.

She knew they would catch her and put her in jail. Her family would have to endure a new humiliation because of her.

She stumbled against a chair and fell. The dim light from the window cast bars across the wall, across her face. A tight band circled her throat, choking her. Noelle tried to scream, but she could manage no more than the hopeless, soundless scream of nightmares.

"Noelle?" The husky male voice against her ear was pleasantly familiar.

Garret had come.

She felt safe. After an eternity of terror.

He would know what to do.

She was aware of the immense comforting shape of him in the darkness. Blindly she reached for him, groped for his granite strength.

"*Chère...*"

His arms had long since gone around her, locking her small body against the bulwark of his. So many times he'd held her like that—as a child, as a woman. She touched his bare muscled back, slid her hands around him and clung to him, trembling uncontrollably in his arms. The band around her throat loosened.

Garret had buried his face in the wealth of her hair. "What's wrong, *chère*?"

Outside it was raining. She was reminded of that long, dark night when the rain had slashed at the hospital window, the night she'd screamed and screamed for him, the night she'd nearly died, the night she'd miscarried their child, the night he'd never come, the night she'd never believed she could forgive him for.

She drew a deep, shaking breath and closed her eyes. "I dreamed...of the robbery again. Only the cops knew I..."

"I have nightmares sometimes, too," he said gently. "Terrible dreams. A crook has me cornered. I pull the trigger, but my gun won't shoot. Or the bullets just roll out of my gun and land at his feet. I never told anybody about those dreams before." Garret ran his hands lightly through her hair.

Her eyes were laden with tears. "Oh, Garret, I've had this same dream every night for a week." Her words were muttered shudderingly against his chest, her hands clutching him. She didn't tell him of the other nightmares.

"I know, *chère*."

"O-only you're never there."

"I'm here now."

She was still trembling, but his grip was tight and comforting.

"What I did at the bank scares me now. I shouldn't have done it. You're in trouble because of me."

"I've been in trouble before."

"I want to go to the captain—"

"No!"

Her mouth was pressed into the hollow of Garret's throat, so she was aware of the exact moment when his pulse quickened abruptly. She licked her lips and involuntarily her tongue flicked against the beating pulse. She felt him tense with excitement.

"Noelle..." he whispered hoarsely, recoiling.

But she ignored his warning. It felt too right to quit.

"Don't push me away," she pleaded against his throat. "You can't go on like this, forever alone...hurting...not letting anybody near." She knew that path—too well. Her lips grazed his throat again. This time deliberately.

She heard the harsh intake of his breath.

"Don't worry about me."

A trembling weakness was spreading through her body. "I can't stop myself."

"Your family, *chère*..."

She caressed his rough cheek with a fingertip. "They don't own me." Her voice was slow, husky, as if with sleep. Her lips kept teasing his skin.

"They damn sure did in the past."

He was on fire. She could feel him shaking everywhere his body touched hers. He wanted her. She knew he did.

"Noelle..." he moaned softly, still determined to resist her.

But she wouldn't let him go when he tried to pull away. "I'm sorry for always making your life harder." Never had she behaved with such boldness. "From now on, I want to make it easier."

He swore inaudibly, but she sensed the beginning of his defeat. His hand had become entangled in her hair. He drew her head back.

There was a long moment of charged silence while he hesitated.

She touched him, sliding a hand down from his throat over the matted hair of his chest. Lower, lower, until his breath came in harsh gasps.

Suddenly she felt his mouth, hard and hot on hers, twisting, hungry, devouring. An agony of mutual need and loneliness were in the urgency of that ravaging kiss. She opened her mouth as his tongue thrust deeply into her mouth. He was bruising her lips, her arms, hurting her, crushing her body into his, but she didn't care. She remembered all the pain, all the despair he'd caused her, but it didn't matter. More than anything she had ever wanted in her short, pampered life, she wanted his fierce lovemaking.

A shiver shot through her like icy fire as he fumbled with the buttons of her dress. She tried to help him, but her dress only shredded beneath their impatient fingers.

"If you aren't more careful, I'll be sending you home naked tomorrow, *chère*," he muttered, nuzzling her breasts with his mouth until they grew taut with pleasure, then trailing hot kisses down to her belly.

She half realized, half feared she'd lit a fire in him that had raged out of control. Her boldness evaporated. "There hasn't been anyone...ever...except you."

"Cut the lies," he muttered ruthlessly. "You were always fickle."

"No..."

"Once I might have believed that. Do you think I care—now?" The angry words were groaned feverishly as he kissed her with long drugging thoroughness.

"Don't kiss me there," she whispered.

"*Chère*, I'm going to kiss you everywhere."

His mouth slid lower. He pulled her panty hose down, while his hand teased her legs open.

"There really hasn't been..."

His hand was inside her, caressing her, turning her senses to flame. "I told you no lies, *chère*. You want this as much as I do. Just don't try to make it into something it isn't." His angry voice was soft, southern, very French.

Then his mouth pressed hot wet woman flesh, and a burning heat radiated through her, its source centered on that intimate place where Garret's mouth was lodged.

Panicked, desperate with the need to escape him if he really believed she was as low as he said, she bucked and writhed. "No..." Her silken hair was crushed and pulling painfully beneath her twisting head. "Please..."

One steel fist caught her hands and locked them together tightly until his mouth persuaded her with his fierce expertise to stop fighting him.

Soon she was no longer capable of rational thought, no longer capable of fighting. What he was doing aroused waves of unbelievable pleasure. He kissed her until she was quivering at the point of ecstasy. Until her body was molten gold against his mouth. Only then did he stop and readjust his great body on top of hers. She caught her breath, afraid to move, spellbound by the exquisite torture of being covered by his lean-muscled sprawl.

Suddenly she felt him tense. He leaned across her, opened a drawer, fumbled with a foil wrapper.

Slowly, with difficulty, he entered her. She arched her back, stiffening. She was tight from two years of abstinence. She bit her tongue to keep from making a sound.

But he knew.

She felt him start in astonishment.

"There hasn't been anyone since I left Louisiana and came back," she murmured.

He became still. "Why not? Doing without was hardly your style before."

She twisted her face away. A tense silence enveloped them.

"So you learned your lesson after all the uproar?" His low voice was a husky murmur as his callused fingertip traced the path of a tear. "I find that hard to believe. You were even two-timing me with Raoul."

"There's no use arguing with you. You wouldn't listen before." She lapsed into silence. She had paid with her heart and soul because he hadn't listened, with her baby's life, nearly with her own. He was as determined as ever to believe the worst of her. The strangest thing of all was that she could still want him, more than ever, that she could still hope, that maybe someday he would believe her.

He touched her cheek tenderly.

She ran her fingers delicately over his shoulders and down to his waist, lingeringly over his sinewy muscles. After a long time he moved against her again, but more gently, kissing her lips long and tenderly, until she was reveling in the hard rhythm of his body moving on hers, until never had she felt such intense, mind-dazzling delight as his sweating muscled body straining with hers.

This was what she had wanted the whole time she'd been in exile.

Only she hadn't known it, hadn't dared to admit it even secretly to herself. Not till he'd come into her shop and taken her in his arms.

His hands were closed around her waist, lifting her so that she fitted him even more tightly. His mouth clamped over hers with a tearing groan. Noelle felt a wave of something glorious building, something hot and vital exploding inside her, and she cried out against his mouth.

Her joy brought his, and he buried himself inside her one last time, shuddering as he held on to her.

"I love you," she whispered. "I don't want to, but I do. You're stubborn, blind, macho. Everything is black-and-white with you. You're always on the defensive because of my family and my money. You've never believed in me. I nearly died . . . But I still love you."

She felt him tense. "I don't mind the insults, but for God's sake, leave the past and the love bit out." He said nothing more as she drifted into sleep in his arms.

Only vaguely was she aware of him letting her go some time during the night. Of him arising. Of him leaving her abruptly to sleep alone.

The rich aroma of gumbo simmering on Garret's stove filled the house. Cooking was a pain, but it was something a man had to do if he lived alone. His Cajun mama had cooking in her blood. She'd taught him how. Maybe that was why he hated it—because he'd done too damn much of it.

Garret had a headache from the whiskey and a queasy feeling in his gut, but it wasn't his headache or his stomachache that was bothering him as he scrubbed the floor furiously where he'd tracked in mud.

Dammit to hell! He should have shown more control last night, but the minute Noelle had touched him, he'd lost his head. Dear God, she'd been good, the first good thing in the past two years.

I love you, she'd said.

How could she say that now? But those words, her sweet trusting voice had haunted him all night long.

She was still the same damn liar she'd always been. She still clung to her story that he was wrong about Raoul, and for some reason Garret almost believed her. And that only proved one thing—that Garret Cagan was the same gullible fool he'd always been when it came to Noelle Martin.

He wasn't going to think about it, about her. It was wrong how wonderful she'd felt. A betrayal somehow. Last night was a mistake. Nothing more. She'd come to his house, crawled into his bed. He'd only given her what she'd begged him for. That was all she'd ever wanted from him. He owed her nothing. Nothing. As soon as she woke up, he had to get rid of her, fast, this time for good.

But it seemed he couldn't keep thinking about her. He couldn't stop remembering how sweet she'd been. How sexy. He remembered how soft and lush her breasts had been when he'd fondled them with his palms. She had the smoothest, warmest flesh—everywhere. Why couldn't he stop thinking of her lying on the other side of that door, alone in his bed? Why couldn't he stop thinking about how good it would feel to slide in beside her and take her again?

The seconds ticked by like hours.

How long was she going to sleep anyway?

After she'd seduced him, he'd spent the rest of the night on his couch without blankets. It had been a cold and comfortless bed, with the buttons of the cushions digging into his bare skin, with his thoughts turning constantly to her. But since his sheets, pillows and blankets were all in the bedroom where she'd been sleeping, he hadn't dared go after them for fear he would succumb to the temptation of getting into bed with her again.

Damn. Two more hours passed. He worked all morning, and still she didn't get up. He finished making the gumbo. He cleaned up the pirogue and the dock, washed his truck. But the whole time he thought only of her. It was almost noon when he decided to force the issue.

He opened his bedroom door with anger in his heart, but his throat constricted at the sight of her. There she was, her lush body curled innocently into a ball, her knees tucked up to her chest, her tousled hair spread across his pillows like silken flames. It was the childlike position Louis always slept in. She looked young and vulnerable and yet more gloriously beautiful than he had ever imagined.

Noelle naked—all curves, pale skin, and long, slender legs. He could not but admire the voluptuous swell of her hips, the graceful thighs, the narrow waist, all the charms that only last night had been his. He wanted nothing more than to go to her, to caress the gently curving back, to feel the warmth of her skin, to know the exquisite joy of her melting into him again. And he despised himself for being such a weak bastard.

Why couldn't she have been poor? Then her family would have looked up to him.

He banged the door shut behind him. She jumped up, startled, fear in her eyes until she recognized him. She smiled drowsily, her eyes lit with a gentle, trusting joy. She didn't bother to cover her naked body that was completely exposed to his gaze. There were black marks on her neck. Another bruise on her shoulder.

His stomach tightened as he remembered what an animal he'd been.

"Did I hurt—"

Damn stupid question. Of course, he'd hurt her. He'd been so hungry for her, he'd been rough as hell. He felt remorse at that.

"I'm sorry. I never meant for any of it to happen," he said. Despair made his voice harsh. "It was a mistake."

Her face whitened. She tried to speak, but no words came out. Enormous golden eyes stared at him with quiet hurt.

He couldn't stand that look in her eyes, so he went to his closet, ripped one of his work shirts off a hanger, and threw it at her.

"Here, put that on, for God's sake."

Though it was the hardest thing he had ever done, he forced his eyes back to her tortured face. He watched her as she fumbled to cover herself with his shirt. Half-dressed, with her tumbled hair and immense eyes, she seemed even sexier than before. She kept brushing her tangled hair off her face with her hand, but the thick, unruly waves kept falling back.

His pulse began beating abruptly in his throat.

"Noelle..."

She looked up at him and then flushed crimson, seeming breathless, flustered, suddenly embarrassed.

As embarrassed as he was.

"About last night," he began awkwardly.

"Don't," she whispered.

"What?"

"Don't ruin it," she began in a faint, whispery voice. "You don't have to tell me to go. I know you didn't want me. Not really. There's no need to despise yourself for what happened. It wasn't your fault. I—I never meant for it to happen, either. I just came out here because I was worried about you.''

"You told me that last night."

"I don't blame you if you don't believe me," she said.

"It was my fault," he muttered angrily, feeling responsible, not wanting to.

She lifted her chin. "And I won't come back. You don't need to worry about me throwing myself at you again."

Odd, how her pride, how her putting it like that, how her acceptance made everything so much more difficult.

"Okay."

She stood, looking rumpled and unbelievably sexy in his shirt, which fell only halfway to her knees, blushing again every time he glanced at her.

He felt a surge of wild excitement.

She picked up her torn dress.

All he saw was white silk flowing against scarlet fingernails. She had beautiful hands.

"Hey, you can't go home in that."

At the sound of his voice, she jumped. The dress slid through her fingers.

She leaned down to pick it up. He bolted to retrieve it at the same time.

"Your father would kill me if..."

Their hands touched.

They both froze.

Their faces lifted and Garret found himself once more staring into her marvelous golden eyes, this time at close range. They were deep and clear, luminous, nervously elegant eyes, dramatically dark centered and black-lashed, fiery with some unfathomable emotion. The memories of last night, of other nights, were still too provocatively vivid in his mind. He remembered her passion, her extraordinary sensuality, and he felt his manhood stir with new life.

For two years he'd told himself he'd rather be dead than ever get involved with her again.

Well, she was here. He was involved. And for the first time in two years, being alive felt almost good.

There was a long moment of silence.

Dammit! If he didn't get rid of her, and quickly, it was going to happen all over again.

Ruthless he shoved her away from him. "You got what you wanted last night, *chère*. Just put something on. Get something out of my closet. Anything. Just get dressed and get out of my life! I don't want you here. Last night didn't change anything!"

But he was wrong, and deep in his bones he knew it.

She gulped in a long, shuddering swallow of air. "You bastard," she whispered. "I'm sorry about last night, too! Sorrier than I've ever been about anything!" Then she ran blindly into the bathroom and slammed the door.

He was in his den feeling like the worst and most loathsome heel ever when she came out of his bedroom nearly an hour later. He pretended to read a newspaper, but the words were a meaningless blur.

She was wearing a pair of his jeans, rolled up at the cuffs and his oversize shirt. He didn't look up, so he didn't see her go over to his stove until it was too late. She grabbed his hot pads.

"Not my gumbo!" he cried, leaping out of his chair, knocking it over, and then stumbling over it. Newspaper pages went flying.

She took the lid off the pot and splashed the gumbo into the sink just as he limped into the kitchen.

"Damn your gumbo!"

She dropped the pot into the sink with a clunk. Then she turned, lifted her chin and stared straight into the blaze of his black eyes, daring him to do something about her outrageous behavior.

He hated cooking. It was so much trouble. He'd fished all night for those crabs and fish. He'd burned the roux once and had to start over. She was so rich and spoiled she was used to sleeping until noon. She'd probably never cooked a damn thing in her life. All of his frustrations became centered on that pot of gumbo gurgling down the sink. He had an overpowering impulse to hurt her, to punish her as if she were a child.

"I ought to beat the hell out of you for that!" he yelled, glaring at her.

She just glared back at him. "Why don't you, then?"

His eyes darkened as they took in the flaming disarray of her hair, the satiny texture of her skin. His gaze trailed down the length of her throat. Too much skin. He could see the shadowy place between her breasts. She wasn't wearing a bra. And why the hell hadn't she buttoned her shirt all the way up?

Dammit. He didn't dare touch her.

Because if he did, he wasn't sure he could stop. He felt a treacherous, unforgivable excitement rising in him. His entire body was shaking. Why did she arouse such uncontrollable passions in him? Hate? Desire? Other unwanted emotions, too.

Suddenly he knew that what he wanted more than anything was to seize her, to slam her against the kitchen counter and make love to her.

"Just get out," he muttered in a voice that sounded hard and filled with hate.

"I'm going as fast as I can, you ungrateful snake. I wish I'd never known you. All you've ever been to me is heartache. Because of you, I hurt my family.... I wish I'd never come out last night to try to help you. Never crawled into your bed again, as you so nastily put it. I hope they take away your gun.... I hope they take away your badge ... and..."

"I get the picture."

"But as much as I hate you," Noelle whispered, "I am sorry about Louis. I never meant to hurt him."

She turned away.

"You think saying that makes it okay, don't you?" His pulse was pounding with anger and with some other emotion he didn't want to put a name to.

He heard the door bang. He heard her footsteps, light and swift, as she raced across his porch. A car door slammed. And suddenly he didn't want her to go.

A minute later he ran out of his house yelling her name. "Come back here, damn you!"

She was already in her car, with her tinted windows rolled up, her doors locked.

For one instant their eyes met. His face was a dark mask of anger. Her eyelids fell. He saw a single tear glistening on her cheek. She seemed to be taking a great interest in her dashboard.

He ran down the porch steps after her. She let him almost catch her. Then she slammed her car into reverse, backing toward him so fast that he had to jump out of her way. Then her tires swerved on oyster shell, slinging loose shells and white mud all over his jeans as she gunned the engine and raced away through that dark, wet tunnel of trees.

Five

___

Even though Garret was bone tired from an eighteen-hour day at Mannie's, and the hour's drive home, he couldn't sleep. He lay propped on his side in his bed staring moodily out his window at the eerie, moss-draped cypress trees. He wasn't thinking of the mountains or Redfish Joliet Rouge and Crawfish Etouffée—that evening's specials—dishes he himself had prepared because the cook had come to work so drunk she couldn't tell a green pepper from a garlic clove. Nor was his mind on his throbbing fingers that were blood raw from peeling what had seemed like a million pounds of boiled, needle-sharp crawfish.

No, Garret was thinking of a society column that had casually mentioned Noelle and Beaumont as a hot item. Even though Garret had shredded the newspaper and thrown it into the fire after reading it, he couldn't forget it. It had made him remember the night she'd come out here; it made him remember how soft and sweet she'd felt under him again. And every time Garret even thought of that rich, snotty wimp, Beaumont Vincent, touching Noelle, Garret felt violent.

Damn Noelle for grabbing that stolen money in the bank! For coming out here and crawling into his bed! Why didn't things ever change for him? Why couldn't he ever learn? If he'd never gone to the French Quarter, or, if even he'd just walked out when she'd started crying in his bedroom, maybe he wouldn't be going through this now.

Garret rolled over, shut his eyes and then opened them again. But all he saw was Noelle, naked in his bed. He kept remembering all the things Noelle had done to him in this very room. His thoughts made him groan aloud and then punch a fist into his pillow. He was determined to hate her, but every night when he'd climbed into bed, for six weeks, he'd tortured himself with the memories of her, tortured himself until his loins were hot and tight with desire for her.

He'd thrown her out of his house, but he hadn't been able to erase her from his heart and mind. He remembered how she'd quivered when his mouth had traced exploring kisses all over her body, how she'd whimpered with those little moans of ecstasy when he'd gotten her thoroughly aroused. She'd been hotter for him than any woman ever had been.

She was rich. She belonged to Beaumont, to her own world of glitter and wealth. Two years ago she'd taught him once and for all exactly what her priorities were, and Garret knew he had better forget about her. It wasn't as if he hadn't tried. He'd let his mother take the first real vacation she'd had in years just so he'd have to work day and night at Mannie's.

The telephone rang, and Garret bolted out of his bed instantly, completely awake. He grabbed the receiver.

"Cagan here...." Garret lay back against his headboard feeling hot and stiff, on edge.

It was Thibodeaux, his supervisor. Since Garret's suspension, he hadn't heard much from him. Only this morning Thibodeaux had called the restaurant and said the investigation wasn't going so well for him.

Thibodeaux's voice had that charged, uptight sound that meant something was wrong. "Good news, Cagan."

"You don't sound like it."

"Well, I know I told you things were stacked against you."

"What happened?"

"Your girlfriend came in and had a long talk with the captain."

Garret's grip tightened on the receiver. "My what?"

"Miss Martin told the captain that you and she were involved. She made the captain understand why you went crazy when you realized she was up there in danger, why you had to disobey orders."

Anger flashed through Garret. Didn't she understand how serious what she'd done was? With the captain, she was way out of her league.

"What did the captain do to her?" Garret muttered in a low, furious voice.

"All I know is that your vacation's over, pal."

"Vacation hell! I've been running Mannie's all by myself for six damn weeks! The cook quit." Nobody but Garret could appreciate how bad that was.

"And come Monday you're going to cry all the way to the bank. I wish I had something besides this job to get by on. You probably don't care whether you're a cop or not."

"The hell I don't. On nights like tonight I think I'd rather starve than ever fry another frog leg."

"There's something else that might interest you."

"What?"

"Tonight, less than an hour ago, someone attacked Evangeline Martin outside her house in the Garden District. She was pretty shaken up when she phoned the police. Then before my patrolman could get over there, Noelle Martin called in and canceled the call."

Evangeline was Noelle's younger sister.

"I'll go by and check things out."

"Noelle Martin said she didn't want us. She mentioned you by name."

"I'll just bet she did."

"What?"

"I'm going to drop in on her anyway."

"Stubborn as ever. Watch your step, Cagan. I get the idea the senator's not too crazy about you."

Garret took his gun out of his nightstand drawer and turned it over, not really seeing the way the gray metal flashed in the moonlight. Instead he saw the wild, crushed look of hurt and anger in Noelle's eyes when he'd told her to get out of his house. He remembered how she'd swallowed and then hidden herself in his bathroom for nearly an hour.

Suddenly he felt an overwhelming urge to stand between her and anything that might threaten her—even himself. It was a ridiculous, crazy feeling. But he felt it just the same.

She'd told him the bank robber would be coming back for the money. She hadn't been afraid of the guy. Once before Garret had underestimated a danger, and Annie was dead because he had. Eva had been assaulted—by someone. Maybe this kid wasn't the sweet, innocent guy Noelle had thought he was. Maybe he was a lot more dangerous.

Garret frowned. Maybe she needed him more than she knew.

* * *

Brakes squealed. A muffler roared and then died as an immaculate white truck rolled to a stop in front of the two-storied, white-pillared, uptown mansion on St. Charles Avenue that was decorated with Christmas lights. A police car was parked discreetly across the street.

Inside her upstairs bedroom, Noelle studied Eva's bruised face.

"Mon Dieu..." This was a sigh of utter despair. Noelle was sitting on the edge of her bed, shivering in the green velvet gown she'd worn to Beaumont's Christmas party. She buried her face in her palms. "I promised him money, but believe me, darling, I never thought he'd pull something this desperate. He seemed so poor and lonely—so alone."

"Only you would try to nab a bank robber, become his hostage, and then befriend him."

"If he'd hurt you, I'd never forgive myself. What did I do to deserve..."

"Look, you're a lot more scared than I am. I'm okay. There's nothing to worry about."

Noelle's throat felt tight and dry, hot with fear at the thought of Eva being hurt.

Ever since Garret had called, Evangeline had been standing expectantly at the massive window, waiting with her older sister. Evangeline's steadiness, her calmness had had a soothing effect on Noelle. Still, Noelle didn't feel up to facing Garret.

Evangeline was pretty, despite the dark bruise on her cheek, but her prettiness lacked the dazzling quality of Noelle's. Eva had red hair, too, but her eyes were dark brown instead of gold. Tonight she was wearing her thick brown glasses as well. She always said she wore her glasses when she wanted to look smart and competent; she wore her contacts when she wanted to look more feminine. Most of the time now—ever since Raoul had vanished from her life—she wore her glasses. She was model slim and she had a penchant for adventure that was more than a match for her older sister.

"Life is always so exciting when you're home, *chère*. Why, imagine, being lucky enough to get entangled with a bank robber."

"Lucky?" Noelle gazed at her sister's bruise. "It was the stupidest thing I've ever done!"

"Oh, I wouldn't say that. I could make a long list of your—"

"Eva!"

Outside the truck door slammed. Evangeline lifted the lace curtains excitedly and saw the tall, broad-shouldered detective in his London Fog raincoat emerge and stride up the sidewalk. He'd called the senator and told him he was coming over with a patrolman. There'd been a quarrel, but they were expecting him. The patrolman got out of his car and joined Cagan. The two men began to talk under a tree that twinkled with Christmas lights.

"Detective Cagan's here," Eva whispered, pushing her overlarge glasses up her nose, and leaning closer against the windowpanes.

"Eva, get back. He'll see you!"

"Thank goodness he didn't drive up in his patrol car with his lights blazing and siren screaming. At least *Grand-mère* won't have anything to explain to the neighbors."

Grand-mère was the least of Noelle's worries at the moment. She was blushing and scared all over again at the thought of facing Garret. She'd rather be attacked by ten bank robbers than see him again. "Well, he couldn't have upset me any more if he had," she muttered.

"You've got to get a grip on yourself."

"I won't see him. I told Papa I wouldn't."

"For two years you were dying to see him."

"That was before..." Noelle's voice trailed off misera-
bly. She remembered the way he'd made love to her and
then humiliated her by throwing her out six weeks ago. If
he'd just called afterward...just once...to wish her Merry
Christmas, anything to show he'd cared.

"Before what?"

Noelle remembered throwing his gumbo down the drain,
nearly hitting him with her car. She'd been hurt, but she'd
behaved badly, like a child who wanted something and
couldn't have it. There could be no doubt that he despised
her.

Noelle blushed. "Nothing."

"I bet nothing was something mighty interesting."

Their eyes met.

"It always is with you, *chère*. All your life your desire to
help has gotten you in trouble."

That was the truth. This morning the captain had said he
was tempted to charge her. Noelle still didn't understand
why she'd gone to the station and put her own neck on the
chopping block for Garret. It was just that when Beaumont had bragged to her that Garret was going to be fired
and forced to leave New Orleans for good, she'd gone a
little crazy. She'd dashed over to the police station and
blurted out a wild story to save him.

Noelle just glared at Evangeline. "And I bet you're the
nosiest sister a girl ever had."

A telling silence fell between the two sisters.

"He needs a haircut," Evangeline mused. "Or at least a
comb! He always looks like he just climbed out of some
woman's bed."

"Eva!" Noelle blushed.

"Well, he does. Lucky woman. And that wrinkled raincoat needs to go to the dry cleaners. And that tie... But even from this distance, I can't see why you even date Beaumont."

"I told you I don't want to talk about Garret Cagan ever again. Besides, I'm probably going to marry Beau. Everybody says he's perfect for me."

"What do they know?"

"At least he's not like some wild animal that bites your hand off every time you try to do something nice for him."

"You're like me, *chère*. We've always had a way with wild animals." Eva's voice was soft, her eyes shadowed.

"Well, I seem to have lost my touch."

The front doorbell rang, and Pierre went to answer it. The sound of Mama's and Papa's voices drifted up the stairs. They were explaining everything in hushed whispers.

Then came the sound of footsteps on the stairs. The three of them were walking up to Noelle's bedroom. Mama kept up a steady stream of irrepressible chatter.

"Detective Cagan's really too good-looking for a man," Evangeline persisted. "Black eyes, black hair..."

Noelle wadded up her bed sheet. "Sounds like a description of the devil to me."

"Or Prince Charming."

Noelle felt herself blush again. It was so hard, sitting here, waiting for him to come, knowing that he thought she'd thrown herself at him. No doubt he'd be furious about the captain, too. One thing was very sure: she despised herself for what had happened even more than he despised her. She would not beg him for anything—ever again.

After an eternity, his knock sounded on the door.

Evangeline started toward the door.

"Don't..."

When no one answered it, the door was flung open, and Garret's wide-shouldered male form filled the massive doorway. He leaned negligently against the doorjamb, looking indolent and relaxed, yet Noelle knew his muscles were coiled, ready to spring with the swiftness of a predatory jungle cat.

"Don't what, *chère*?" he taunted softly. "Were you planning to order me out of your bedroom?"

Noelle bit back the angry words that would have done just that. She felt her cheeks go hot, and she averted her gaze from his but not without retaining a vivid impression of his rampantly handsome male features. His black hair was too long as Eva had said, but it framed a bronze face so perfect God must have designed it for the single purpose of ensnaring a foolish female heart such as hers. Indeed the mere sight of him made that treacherous organ pound violently against her rib cage.

Noelle stared at him hungrily—ebony hair, black eyes and jet brows, the long straight nose, the high cheekbones, the lean stubborn jaw. And the mouth—so full and sensually shaped, even twisted as it was now in mockery of her. She remembered how marvelous those hard lips had felt on hers. Dear God. She closed her eyes, not wanting to remember.

"Merry Christmas," he murmured.

Noelle stumbled over her own tongue. "D-didn't Papa tell you there was no need for you to come?"

"He told me." The hardness in Garret's dark gaze belied his drawling tone.

Her eyes coolly met his. "Then..."

Garret looked past Noelle to Evangeline. At the sight of her bruised face, his expression became grimmer. "Miss Martin, if you wouldn't mind," he began gently, "I'd like to speak to your sister for a minute—alone. My patrolman is just outside. He has a few questions. Then I'll talk to you myself."

Garret's manner toward Evangeline was subtly different from his manner toward Noelle. He was more courteous, not so pushy and disrespectful, and Noelle found herself resenting him even more.

"Of course," Evangeline answered politely.

"Eva, don't you dare leave me with him."

Evangeline came to the bed and took her sister's shaking hands in hers. "You'll feel better after you get this over with, and I'll be right outside if you need me."

She left then, and Noelle found herself alone with the one man she'd sworn she'd stay away from.

He stepped into the center of her golden satin and lace bedroom. Never before had she realized how frilly and feminine the room was. Mama loved lacy things and spindly antiques.

"So this is your sanctuary—where you hide from things you're scared of—like me." His eyes roamed the room, taking in her doll collection, her doll furniture collection.

She remembered the Spartan simplicity of his home and furnishings. Her own home was filled with many beautiful but useless items.

Awkwardly he picked up an antique doll and then put it down. His gaze settled on her. "You were always collecting stuff back then. You had these things when you were a child."

"So what if I did."

"This is a little girl's room, not a woman's." The last word was liquid velvet. So were his black eyes. "Why are you so scared to be a woman?" he murmured.

Noelle froze, staring up at him from the bed. Legs spread apart, he seemed more masculine than ever as he stood on that white carpet in front of her flower drapes and lace sheers.

"I'm not scared of . . . of anything. Not of you, either," she whispered defiantly.

"No?" He shrugged out of his raincoat and draped it over a gold damask chair, heedless that the water drops might spot the fabric.

He wore a navy suit and a blue tie that didn't quite match. She noticed how the white collar of his shirt emphasized the swarthy shade of his throat and face. His suit tapered from his wide shoulders to his narrow waist and lean hips. His potent masculine virility struck out at her with the force of a body blow.

"But it's a nice room . . . even if it should be a child's," he said, moving closer. "Nice bed. I always think of you in nice rooms . . . and nice beds." He touched the smooth cypress bedposts of the bedstead. "A plantation antique, no?" He said something low, in French. "I remember it from Martin House."

She sprang off the bed, suddenly realizing how intimate it was, receiving Garret in her bedroom.

"It's a favorite piece of mine," she said.

"Mine, too," he whispered.

When she ran to the farthest window, he followed her there. She whirled around, and he was so close she could have reached out and touched him.

"Relax, *chère*, this will only take a few minutes—if you cooperate with me. By the way, thanks. I got my job back."

She arched her brows in surprise. "I'm surprised you're not even madder at me."

"I'm so stubborn, sometimes I don't know how much I value something—until I come close to losing it." His eyes were still brilliant and dark. The statement was made in a smooth, low tone rife with sexual innuendo.

His words and his gaze prodded her to move farther away. "Just go. Send someone else. Anyone but you," she pleaded desperately, wishing he wasn't so tall and broad, wishing he didn't tower over her, wishing she didn't know how wonderful it would feel for her body to melt into his.

A bitter grimace chased across his mouth. "Why not me?"

His compelling gaze met hers. She was aware of a sudden volt of electricity flowing between them, its tingling existence such a tangible thing it couldn't be ignored.

"You know why," she whispered.

"Look, *chère*..."

He seemed too close to her, so Noelle took another half step backward. The hot light in his eyes was making her senses reel.

"Don't call me that. And I don't want to talk about it."

"About coming to my house? Or about what happened to Eva tonight?"

"Neither."

"Then we'll talk about tonight. It was the kid from the bank, wasn't it?"

Noelle bit her lip.

"It's no use—your covering for him. I'm going to catch him sooner or later."

"Why can't you just forget about him?"

"Because he committed a crime."

Garret moved closer, out of the shadows and into the dim, golden glow of the lamp by the window. The light fully illuminated his dark, carved features, and for the first time she noticed that his face, though still handsome, was leaner and more uncompromising than before. Pain and sorrow had carved new lines. The harsh experiences he'd endured had stamped out all softness. He seemed tough and strong, and most of all, unrelentingly masculine.

"Noelle, I'm sorry about the way I acted that night. I've thought about it a lot. Especially after I heard you talked to the captain."

"Don't..."

"I know you don't want me here, but I came tonight because we're in this together. You helped him get away; I helped you. It's our fault if he does something crazy. This could be one disturbed kid. I don't want Evangeline or anyone else hurt. Most of all, I don't want him to hurt you."

"You don't care about me."

"I do care, *chère*." This was said so softly each syllable seemed to quiver down the length of her spine.

"No."

She tried to back away, but he wouldn't let her. He put an arm on either side of her shoulders, imprisoning her. "Listen to me, Noelle..." He touched her cheek. "I'm not very good at this sort of thing."

She twisted her face away, her amber eyes smoldering with outrage. "You never even called!"

"Because of the past. Your family—"

"Forget them! It's you. You're so stubborn you'll never forgive me."

She wouldn't look at him, but never had she been more conscious of a man's nearness. Why was it always like this for her? He had only come into a room, and her thoughts, her heart, her soul focused on him.

As always he had an uncanny sense of what she was feeling.

"Maybe I've got no choice but to try, *chère*. There hasn't been a day I didn't think about you, nor a night. I kept remembering the way you smelled—like those wild roses. The way you tasted—like tart honey. The way you felt...better than any other woman had ever felt to me before. I didn't call because I know I can never fit into your world. But some nights, like tonight, when I lie in bed all alone without sleeping and start thinking about you, I wonder if you're ever as lonely without me as I am without you."

The image of him longing for her was treacherously tantalizing. His hands were in her hair, sifting through the bright strands. She felt his fingers on her neck, gently circling her slender throat. He was so close she could feel the warmth of his body. She inhaled the musky, unforgettable, intoxicating scent of him.

"Stop it! And don't touch me. I don't believe you."

The sudden tightening of his jaw told her he was working hard to control his temper.

"I went crazy when I thought that bastard came here, that he might have hurt you."

"You just want to catch him because they blamed you for letting him get away. No, I don't believe—"

"Then believe this, you little fool!" Garret muttered savagely, his patience at an end.

Roughly he snapped her against his body until every muscular inch was pressed against her, capturing her frantic hands that tried to push him away, and twisting her arms behind her back.

"If I scream, they'll throw you off the case."

"Then I'll have to find a way to stop you from screaming."

He covered her mouth with his. When she struggled, his arms became a vise, his fingers raking into her fiery hair, holding her neck, stilling her twisting head, forcing her lips to remain beneath his.

Noelle fought him, but his hands used her every movement to mold her body more fully to his. She felt his fingers slide across her breasts. Her hips were crushed into the wall by his rock-hard thighs. She felt the stiff leather edges of his concealed holster press into her chest as he ravaged the softness of her lips.

Despite her past humiliation and her resolve never to respond to him again, her body betrayed her. His mouth and hands evoked pleasures so intense she could not keep them secret from him. All too soon she was trembling with the strange and wonderful sensations she'd told herself she'd never let herself feel again.

The minute Garret felt her resistance begin to ebb, his own anger melted. The hardness of his arms around her and the pressure of his mouth lessened imperceptibly. With a convulsive movement, she arched her body against his.

Freeing her mouth he lowered his black head, trailing hot kisses down her throat.

"No," she gasped weakly.

His breath was deep and harsh, and he ignored her pleas as if he hadn't heard them, his warm mouth kissing the soft green velvet that covered her breasts until the fabric became damp and hot, until her own breath became tiny gasps, until her pulse was racing out of control.

"Garret, stop. You have to stop." But even as she pleaded, she was only an instant away from total surrender.

His fingers were on the zipper of her dress. He was just as close to the edge as she was. Suddenly he pushed her away from him with a shudder and stepped back, leaning against the wall, breathing heavily, combing both his hands through his black hair.

Every nerve in her own body was quivering as she watched him.

She kept studying him, dazed, as he loosened his awful tie.

"That tie's not right for your suit," she whispered. "It's royal blue. You suit's navy."

"What?"

"I said—"

"I heard," he muttered, grinning, looking sheepish. "I never was much good at matching colors. It was blue, so I thought . . ."

His obvious embarrassment charmed her.

"I—I'll have to go shopping with you sometime."

"I'd like that, *chère*."

They were speaking like any ordinary couple.

Suddenly she was in his arms, of her own volition, pressing her head tightly into his muscular shoulder, holding on to him, feeling safe and protected as she only did when he was near, safe enough to blurt it all out.

"Oh, Garret, it was awful. I wanted you to come. Only you. But I didn't because . . . I'd gone to your house and thrown myself at you."

"I know." He petted her hair. "Tell me everything, *chère*."

Her hand inadvertently touched the hard bulge of his gun beneath his coat, and she drew her hand back.

"Eva was coming home when he jumped her. He thought she was me. He wanted money. Oh, Garret, he said he was coming back."

For a long while Garret held her tightly, comforting her in grim silence.

At last he spoke. "You've got to help me get him, Noelle."

"No."

"There's no one else."

"I'm leaving town tomorrow," she said quickly, "and taking Eva with me."

"What?"

"There's an estate sale in Mobile. Then we're flying back to Baton Rouge. There are several antique dealers along the

River Road between Baton Rouge and New Orleans we always visit this time of year. Then there's Christmas. The whole family will celebrate the holiday at Martin House.''

"When will you be back?"

"After Christmas, I've decided to go to Europe—to buy antiques for the shop."

He set Noelle away from him slowly. His cutting gaze slashed her. "You little coward. You're running away, and you don't care about anybody but yourself." He grabbed her again, and she felt his harsh grip digging into her skin.

"He only wants to see me!"

"How do you know? I made the mistake of thinking that way once! Annie's dead because I did. Your friendly bank robber attacked Eva."

Even though Garret was hurting her, Noelle didn't try to pull free. "But don't you see? The reason I'm going is to take her with me. You're a good cop. You have a hundred men under you. You'll have to find him without me."

"Send Eva to buy antiques in Europe. I need you, Noelle."

Her heart leaped, but as she searched his hard face, she did not find even the slightest trace of tenderness.

"For what?" she whispered desperately.

His dark eyes were flat and cold. He only wanted to catch the thief and clear his own name.

A stone was in her heart, weighing it down.

"You don't care about me," she said.

"I'm a cop. I've got a job to do. It's my fault Eva got attacked tonight. Yours, too. You owe me."

"In the shop you said I would owe you nothing."

"I made a lot of mistakes in the shop. We have to catch this guy."

"He's only a boy. A poor boy." *A boy who reminds me of Louis.* But she did not say that.

"I know a hell of a lot more about poor boys than you do. They grow up in jungles. Jungle creatures will do anything to survive."

"You're too hard."

He was unmoved by her words. "I can't change what I am, *chère*." He spoke with icy calm. "No matter how I might want to. No matter what I might feel for you."

"You don't feel anything for me."

"I don't want to. That much is damn sure true."

"You only came tonight because you want to use me." Noelle caught back a sob. "That's why you kissed me. That's why you held me."

He gave her a look that was like a knife wound to her heart. "You think you know so much," he muttered thickly in a raspy sound that suggested pain. "You don't know me at all." Then he turned and stalked toward the door.

She heard it open. She heard it slam.

She looked up when she was sure he'd gone.

The gilded room was empty and cold. Outside in the darkness a wild wind swirled dead, wet leaves and the Christmas lights blinking in them.

She shivered.

She had disappointed Garret. Again.

For some reason, knowing that hurt most of all.

Six

―――

"What's *he* doing here?"

The words were frail and thin like the woman who had spoken them. Yet despite her fragility, the old lady's black eyes were as sharp as ever, darting everywhere, missing nothing.

With an imperious gesture Marlea Martin used a gnarled finger to push her bifocals higher up the bridge of what Garret Cagan had once labeled "the haughtiest nose in New Orleans."

At the tension radiating in her grandmother's voice, Noelle glanced up, a frown on her lovely face. She'd been overseeing the loading of her luggage and Eva's into the Martin jet.

Even though Noelle and Eva were only flying to Mobile and then on to Baton Rouge and Martin House, Bibi had insisted the girls take the jet.

Hunching precariously over her silver cane, Marlea was a frail birdlike figure in black silk—Noelle had never seen her in any other color. No longer did Marlea seem the formidable matriarch who had raised Noelle almost single-handedly. Dear *Grand-mère*. The slightest upset these days could send her to bed for weeks. Noelle looked past her grandmother into the drizzle and saw the tall, dark man in a leather jacket and jeans. He was loping toward the Martin's private hangar.

"Garret..." The sight of him, a lonely, forlorn figure in the rain, touched some wellspring deep within Noelle. Her frown deepened as she told herself that feeling was no more than a lingering weakness she was determined to deny. Nevertheless, her carryon slowly slipped through her fingers onto the concrete.

Wade Martin and Beaumont Vincent, who'd come to see Noelle off, too, grew rigid at the sight of him. Her father was a small man, about five feet eight, but his facial expression, his bold black eyes so like his mother's, and the set of his large head and thick neck gave the impression of greater size and power.

Noelle started to go to Garret. Then she caught her father's warning glance and Beau's scowl. Her grandmother was looking pale and shriveled all of a sudden as if the mere sight of Garret was too much for her. For some idiotic reason, Noelle felt pulled in two directions.

The older woman's alarm infected Noelle, and she suddenly felt frightened, too, as she remembered how precarious her grandmother's health was.

"*Grand-mère!* Papa! You don't have to say anything, any of you. I'll go out and talk to him."

"Stay away from him," Wade commanded. "You know your grandmother isn't well."

"I'm not a child." Noelle swallowed. "And no matter what any of you think, Garret Cagan is not a bad man."

At this rebellion Marlea faltered. The silver cane clattered to the concrete.

Noelle knelt and picked it up and put it into her grandmother's shaking fingers. "Try to understand," Noelle said gently, stroking the thin, age-spotted hand. "He won't go unless I speak to him."

Then she ran out into the rain.

Garret stopped moving when he saw her. He'd been filled with anger, despair, utter hopelessness until he caught sight of Noelle running toward him. Suddenly he was transfixed by her translucent beauty.

The wind blew her hair, and fiery tendrils flew against her brow and flushed her cheeks. Her lush breasts heaved gently beneath her tight, mint-green sweater. Cashmere, he imagined. Her wool skirt was the same color. A chic gold necklace was knotted at her throat. There was more gold at her wrists, but not too much. Behind her the wind was whipping up whitecaps on the surface of Lake Pontchartrain.

Noelle stopped just before she reached him. They devoured each other with their eyes. He did not know what she was feeling, but he felt the blood rush to his face. For him, she was like a sexual magnet. It didn't matter that her family was there regarding him with dark looks of disdain. It didn't matter what she'd done. If only he could have her again. Dear God. And again.

Maybe he had a tough exterior, but on the inside, when it came to her, he was weak.

He smiled warily, wishing things were different, and that Noelle would come flying into his arms. He wanted to hold her, to never let her go.

Garret hesitated, feeling awkward, not knowing what to say, too aware of the clumped dark shadows in the hangar, the members of the Martin family standing like stiff sentinels, watching them—too aware of Noelle's deepening frown.

Garret remembered that long night in the hospital when Noelle had nearly died. The Martins had sat in the waiting room together; he'd stood in the hall outside because they couldn't endure his presence any nearer to them. They'd blamed him for everything; their feelings had only intensified his own feelings of guilt and terror as he'd waited to learn whether Noelle would live or die.

The wind was blowing Noelle's hair and dampening her green wool sweater.

"Hey," Garret said gently after a long time. "Let's get you out of the rain."

She nodded awkwardly, and he led her by the hand into the hangar.

Her family viewed him the way they always did—as though they were superior beings and he were an especially grotesque member of some inferior, much-despised species. In the past Garret would have tensed and greeted them with the same silent contempt they showed him. But today, even though their hostility put him on edge, he forced himself to speak politely to each of them, meeting their eyes, smiling at them when they mumbled something awkwardly. He went to the regal old lady in black and took her thin, palsied hand, holding it for a long moment as if to impart some of his strength to her.

"You're looking well, Mrs. Martin. Better than when I last saw you. I'm glad," Garret said. "I always blamed myself for everything that happened."

Just for a second he thought he felt her cling to his fingers before she remembered herself and abruptly pulled it free of his grasp.

"As well you should, Garret Cagan," Marlea rasped.

Garret offered his hand to Beaumont and Wade. For an endless moment he towered over the two men, his hand suspended in the air. When Garret realized they weren't going to take it, he went white for a few seconds. Quickly he recovered himself and dropped his hand.

The Martins sensed a change, and they felt ill at ease. All except Eva and Mama.

"It's nice your detective came to see you off, no, *chère*?" Bibi exclaimed, stirring the pot of drama.

The senator's glare at his incorrigible wife held the same quiet embarrassment that his mother's did, but Bibi merely ignored her mother-in-law and laughed lightly at her husband.

"Thank you, Mama. But he's not my detective. And he certainly didn't come to see me off."

"I should hope not," Beaumont said, thunderstruck.

Eva stepped out of the plane and waved warmly at Garret.

"Noelle, the pilot is ready for departure," Wade said coldly. "Cagan, I warned you two years ago to stay away from my daughter. Though I allowed you into my house the other night, it was as a detective, not as a suitor."

"Papa!"

Garret ground his teeth together. He could feel a muscle ticking furiously at his jawline. This whole situation was impossible. He turned to speak to Noelle. His tone was cool but polite. "We'll just be a minute, sir. I need to talk to Noelle. It's official police business."

"Official police business, hell!" Beaumont stormed, flushing darkly. "Noelle, you don't have to talk to him."

Garret didn't like Vincent's tone when he spoke to Noelle. It was as if he thought he had some proprietary right over her and could tell her how to act.

"Go ahead and talk to him, *chère*," Bibi said.

Garret ignored them all and swept Noelle into a tiny office where they could be alone, but the door had a window in it.

His hand closed over her forearm. "You have the most amazing family. They seem equally divided. Half of them love me. Half of them hate me."

"I know the feeling," she whispered bitterly.

"The question is—which half is running the show?"

She met his gaze with blazing eyes, and he thought he knew her answer. Garret looked out the window and saw Vincent pacing back and forth, and the thought of Beaumont even touching Noelle made Garret angrier. "Just what kind of relationship do you have with Vincent, anyway?"

Her chin lifted defiantly. "That's none of your business."

Garret's hand clamped around her wrist, pulling her closer. He felt the shock of touching her go through his whole body. "Are you really going to marry him?"

She eyed him levelly and said nothing for a long moment. "I wonder if that would matter to you at all."

"Just tell me this, *chère*—are you sleeping with him, too?" His fingers became a vicious vise, and their brutal pressure jerked her toward him.

"Damn you," she whispered. He felt her recoil. "I . . ." She glared up at him.

He stood there like a statue and stared her down. Instinctively he knew the exact second when her rage bubbled over, the exact second when she tensed to strike him.

He caught her hand before it could complete the swinging arc and make violent contact with his hard cheek.

"Does that mean yes or no?" he demanded coldly.

"It means..." She hesitated, her indignant gaze locked with his.

He thought that she enjoyed dangling him on the cruel hook of her silence. With every hushed second that passed, she set the hook deeper until he felt a tearing pain as if every cell in his body ached for her to say no. A mindless rage at himself that this was so began to pulse within him.

He was the first to break.

"Look," he began raggedly, "it does matter to me. I know Vincent can give you things, a life, everything..." The huge knot in Garret's throat made it impossible for him to go on.

She was watching him closely, expectantly, reading him. "No, he can't give me...everything," she admitted at last, very softly. Gently she pulled her hand free of his so that she could caress the top of his lean bronzed wrist. "But, it is true that Beau can give me what *Grand-mère* and Papa want for me, what any normal woman would want—a safe, predictable, respectable life. I owe *Grand-mère* so much. You know...that because of me...because of us...she had that stroke. She couldn't talk...for nearly six months while I was away in Australia. I don't want to hurt her like that ever again. It would be a lie if I said I haven't been thinking about marrying Beau, but, no, I'm not sleeping with him."

Convulsively Garret's fingers tightened on Noelle's. He pulled her hard against him. Her head only came to his chin; he felt her lips pressed into the hollow of his throat. "Don't then. Wait." After a long tense moment of holding her close, he let her go, kissing her gently on the brow.

He cupped her chin tenderly. Then both hands moved to frame her face.

His hand traced Noelle's delicate jawline. The feel of her skin was insidiously erotic. He remembered their forbidden nights together on his boat, in his house, other places; nights when they had lain awake for hours, holding each other in different embraces, their passion burning between them like wild flames of desire. He had stored a lifetime of memories.

Abruptly he let her go.

"Why did you come here, Garret?" The light in her eyes bathed him with flaming heat.

"Because I couldn't leave things the way they were between us last night. I was too rough," he murmured. "I . . . I'm sorry I didn't call you after that night you came out to my house. I know how hard it must have been for you to go there. But, you see, I thought it was over—this thing between you and me. I wanted it to be over."

Her beautiful face was filled with warmth and compassion.

He continued. "I want you to come back—not just to help me catch that crazy punk. But back—to me."

"What?"

"I know everything went wrong before. I can promise you nothing." His gaze lifted from her face. He stood there looking straight ahead, out the glass window. The plane was waiting. So was her family and Beaumont. Impatiently. Angrily.

"I'm probably a fool to ask you," he said. "You never dared to date me openly. Maybe we've gone through more than a couple can and survive. You're not the only one with a lot to lose."

Hell, no, she wasn't! He was probably throwing his whole life away, his independence, perhaps Louis in the bargain, everything he'd worked so hard for. His gaze came back to her lush mouth. He was courting fresh disaster, and yet he was totally unable to stop himself.

"Only this time," Garret continued in a grimmer tone, "we play by my rules and not yours. No more sneaking around from your family. I won't be your illicit poor-boy lover."

"Oh, Garret, you were never that."

"Wasn't I? You move out of their house...their *houses*. Rent a place of your own, live on the money you make. No more being flown places in the family jet—unless they're along. And you date no one—except me."

"And Louis?"

Garret looked at her and saw the shimmer of tears in her eyes. He glanced away quickly before he softened.

"We'll leave him out of this for now."

"Oh, so I'm supposed to turn my own personal life upside down, and you want your own family protected?"

"We played by your rules before." His gaze was hard as it slashed back to her face. "You always snuck around to see me. That only made your family resent me even more."

"You're asking me to choose between my family and you, when you refuse to make the same choice?"

"No, it's not like that. The last thing I want is to come between you and them. With Louis, it's the opposite problem. He'll get his hopes up all over again if he sees you. He's very fragile. You know how he was after Annie's death. Then you came along, and he adored you. But it cut him up when you left. He retreated into his shell. Only it's almost worse because he's six now. He hasn't spoken a single word... One day he just packed his things and took his pirogue and poled himself through the swamp all the way back to Annie's mother's. He hardly...looks at me when I come around."

"But, Garret, aren't there doctors?"

"He's been to all of them. The trauma did something to him. He hates goodbyes. I'm not keeping you away from him to hurt you. I just can't risk Louis. That's all."

She took a shaky breath. "But I'm supposed to risk everything?"

"I know it's a lot, *chère*. Probably too much."

He lifted aside the molten fire of her hair, pushing it away from her neck. "You always said I was a pushy guy, yes?" Then his mouth found the sensitive spot at the base of her throat where he could kiss her pulse.

He touched her pulse first with his tongue and then with his mouth, deepening the kiss only after he felt the tiny throbs skitter crazily. As always he had only to touch her and she was on fire for him. As hot as he was. It didn't matter that she was a cherished princess of Creole aristocracy, and he a cop, the son of a cook and a logger.

Garret's roughened hand slid under her sweater to the back of her waist, but she pulled away.

She leaned breathlessly against the wall. "I can't think when you do that."

"I don't want you to think. I just want you to come back to me," he whispered.

"Why should I when you won't forgive me, when you can't love me?"

"That's going to take time, *chère*."

She looked up, searching his face. "So will my decision," she said finally. "Louis isn't the only one who was hurt before."

Low, harsh laughter erupted from Garret's throat. "You're damned right there."

He was mocking himself, but she thought he was mocking her. She opened the door to rush out of it. But he grabbed her. His mouth curled cruelly.

His arms locked around her with iron force. His lean masculine frame shaped itself against her soft curves. Ten thousand years of civilization died in that hard embrace. He felt primitive, virile, all male. He couldn't let her go. His grip tightened on her wrist.

His velvet tone was a command. "Not so fast, *chère*."

A thrill coursed through him at the heat sparking in her golden eyes.

"This is exactly what's wrong with our relationship—it always gets physical," she whispered.

But he caught the low quiver of excitement in her voice.

"Do you really want to live without it?" he muttered huskily. "Without me? Can you?"

They stared at each other for endless seconds until she flushed. He ran a hand up the side of her arm, across her breast, up her throat, along her windpipe until she trembled from his erotic touching, until she closed her eyes, until she half opened her mouth and bent her head back, her breath coming unevenly. She licked her wet lips, pursed them expectantly.

His mouth lowered within inches of hers. He felt a wild excitement mounting within him, that keen pleasure that was almost like pain, but even though he was on fire with longing, he stopped himself.

"No, *chère*," he whispered thickly. "I'm not going to kiss you. I want you to know exactly what it feels like—to want it, to crave it, and to do without. I want you to lie awake nights and imagine yourself in Vincent's marriage bed—wanting this."

The heat of his body touched hers.

Her eyes snapped open. "Why you—"

He ran a light, electrifying finger across an erect nipple pushing against cashmere, and she jumped back.

"Just remember, *chère*, if you marry that rich, pompous wimp, you'll have him, but you won't have me. Not ever again."

"Maybe I'll be perfectly happy with him!"

"Maybe." He shrugged with seeming indifference. It was a French gesture, cocky, peculiarly his. "Maybe not. After all, you're more your hot-blooded mama's daughter than your blue-blooded father's. You'll never be a true Martin."

"No!"

"Yes. And someday you're going to figure out who you really are. I only hope it isn't too late—for both of us."

Noelle was beginning to shake. She clasped her arms around her body and lowered her head, trying to control the quivering.

Garret reached for her, to take her into his arms and comfort her, but she pushed him away, a sigh shuddering from her lips. "I hate you," she whispered.

"I don't think so."

"I do."

"If you come back to New Orleans, you come back to me, *chère*," he murmured.

His hot, black gaze burned into her.

"T-that is something I can never do, Garret Cagan." She took a last tortured breath, and then she opened the door and ran from him.

His chest filled with a cold, tight lump. Bleakly he watched her as she raced toward her family. Away from him.

Hell. She was only going to Alabama and then on to Baton Rouge. Why did it feel like she was flying to the end of the earth?

He still had the holidays to think of some way to stop her from going on to Europe.

The narrow green skirt sheathed her hips. She had the most perfect body. He felt a sharp stab of desire.

Beaumont opened his arms. Not wanting to see Noelle run into them, Garret ducked his head and pretended to study a jagged crack in the concrete floor. When he looked up, Vincent was empty armed and Noelle had vanished inside the jet.

Ten days later Noelle stood behind the huge white Christmas tree at Martin House and stared moodily at the silver package Eva had secretively handed her after all the other gifts had been opened. It was from Garret.

Even as she told herself passionately that she didn't want to open it, that she wasn't going to open it, she was ripping the bright foil paper and letting the coils of silver ribbon fall heedlessly to the carpet.

There was a note inside. Her fingers tightened convulsively around the package when she saw Garret's bold black scrawl, *Chère, come back to me.*

He had not signed his name, but he didn't need to. After she read the words, his message seemed to echo in her heart.

She opened the small velvet box and gasped with pleasure. Inside was an amethyst pendant set with tiny diamonds. It was so exquisite she was almost afraid to touch it.

Her fingertip traced lingeringly over the fragile gold and glittering stones. He had remembered that amethysts were her birthstones, just as he had remembered how she loved them. The necklace had probably cost much more than he could afford, and yet he had afforded it. A sudden huge lump formed in her throat.

She snapped the box shut and hid it quickly in the pocket of her skirt. There was no way she could rejoin Beau and the others in the dining room, no way she could pretend nothing out of the ordinary had happened.

Quickly she opened a French door and went outside onto the veranda, rushing headlong down the brick paths that wound among the gardens. Through the tangle of live oak, azaleas and thick creepers of lacy jasmine, Martin House was white and lovely in the soft sunshine. The air was redolent with the smell of the swamp, almost cool; the bayou with its floating hyacinths was smooth and placid. But she scarcely noticed the loveliness of the familiar setting.

She touched the velvet box in her pocket. Despite the knowledge that her family and Beau were in the house, loneliness washed over her.

What was she going to do about Garret? Was she going to Europe? Or back to New Orleans? If she returned to the city, Garret would believe she was choosing him.

Choose Garret? On his terms? Never.

She looked up and saw that she had come to the darkest corner of the garden. Martin House was now lost in the jungle of flowers and semitropical greenery.

Nearby on the bayou the sun shone on something gold. She twisted her head and saw that someone was watching her. A scream rose in her throat and then died. Her heart began to thud violently.

A slim blond child with incredibly intense blue eyes had poled his pirogue almost to the edge of the low bank. The boy's yellow hair fell thick and straight across his brow. His thin mouth attempted a smile and quivered instead. In the bow was a plump basset hound dozing as lazily as if it were a summer day and she was secure and safe on dry ground.

An incredible joy that felt like a sudden tearing pain in Noelle's chest filled her as she recognized the boy and his dog.

Garret's child was taller, older; paler and more solemn than she remembered. But she loved him more than ever.

She formed his name on her lips but lacked the voice to speak it.

Louis...

His big blue eyes shimmered with pain and delight. Then his expression changed ever so slightly. He bit his lips, and he glanced away as if he were ashamed of his powerful feelings.

He was holding a clump of something white in his hands—early dogwood blossoms that he probably had found somewhere in the swamp.

With perfect aim he tossed the flowers carelessly through the trees at her. They landed at her feet the way Jess's bridal bouquet had. Slowly she knelt to retrieve the scattered blossoms, picking them up, one by one.

When she looked up, there was only a gleaming ripple where his pirogue had been. Louis had gone.

Had he picked the flowers for her? Had he thrown them to her out of love or bitter despair?

Her entire body ached with the need to call him back, to hold him tightly in her arms. To explain why she had had to tell him goodbye. To never, never, let him go.

She loved him as much as if he were her own. He was Garret's flesh and blood. He could have been hers so easily if she had not been young and foolish, if she had not allowed herself to be so easily manipulated into running away by her family.

She had lost her own baby, and now as Louis poled himself away from her, she felt his loss as keenly as if he were her own child she was losing all over again.

"Louis!"

Her voice was a thin light sound, dying away in the deeply shadowed bayou.

He did not come back.

The overgrown garden seemed a maze of tangled paths. She felt alone, cold and empty. Just as she'd felt when her tiny baby had died. She stared helplessly at the freshly picked white blossoms, but they were blurred by her tears. Her cheeks became wet.

Mon Dieu! Why couldn't she put the child out of her heart?

Why hadn't she ever been able to forget his father? She had been sent away when she was seventeen to do so. Her family had believed Garret was a teenage infatuation, easily forgotten. But instead of forgetting, she had wanted him more than ever after she'd finally ventured back to New Orleans seven years later to be a Mardi Gras queen the same season her sister had also been favored with a crown.

She kept looking at the white flowers, but she was remembering other flowers, another time.

Memories of that special night two years ago when she'd seen Garret again and they had resumed their impossible love affair for the second time came hurtling out of the locked doors in her mind.

Seven

Instead of Louis's dogwood blossoms, Noelle saw again the fragile white orchids that had adorned the Martins' house in the Garden District the night of the ball two years ago. Her memory of the lavish affair was as vivid as though it has occurred only yesterday.

Noelle was back in Louisiana, back in New Orleans for her first Carnival in seven years. She had been away at school. Then she'd studied at Christie's and worked in New York to learn about the antique business. Seven years of running....

The newspapers had proclaimed Noelle the most beautiful Mardi Gras queen of the season, the dazzling queen of Papa's prestigious krewe. Eva was the queen of another but equally prestigious krewe. Every night Noelle had worn a different evening gown. A dozen men were in love with her, but she had halfheartedly promised herself to Beaumont Vincent only because he was rich and handsome and every other girl was dying to marry him, only because Papa and *Grand-mère* approved. Still, every night Noelle recklessly allowed more than a dozen suitors to court her, thus, she created a whirlwind of scandalous excitement wherever she went.

For herself, she was oblivious to the furor she was causing at the parades and balls, oblivious to Beaumont's growing jealousies, indifferent to everything and every man until that night when Papa had thrown that one ball especially for her in their home. Because of a rash of jewel burglaries, and the rumor that the thief had a particularly vicious personality, Papa had hired two off duty plainclothes detectives as guards to protect his home and wealthy guests.

Noelle had been wearing a white beaded gown Mama had found in Paris and Mama's diamonds that night. It was tight and unbearably uncomfortable, because Noelle had always been too much of a tomboy to ever dress up as easily as other girls. A crown of pale orchids gleamed softly in her red hair. She was chattering and laughing and casting quick glances at all her admirers every time Beaumont looked away. Raoul Girouard was one of the few single men not caught in Noelle's web. Instead he was paying an inordinate amount of attention to Eva much to *Grand-mère*'s dismay. Thus, both Martin girls were creating a sensation, each in their own way.

Noelle was breathless from dancing, and yet filled with that same terrible restlessness that had always been a problem to her. Or at least since she'd been seventeen and in love with Garret Cagan.

Noelle didn't feel like dancing. She felt hemmed in by propriety, by all the unspoken rules governing Carnival royalty, and by her family's hopeful expectations. On a whim, Noelle had sent Beaumont to get champagne so she could flirt with Armand. But she felt vaguely bored by Armand, too.

Suddenly her long-lashed eyes had lifted, bright with startled vivacity and met a swarthy man's brooding black gaze.

In the foreground Armand's face blurred. Into sharper focus came the dark, reckless violence of the handsome, hard features of the stranger who was behind them.

Her smile died a fluttery death because the man was no stranger.

He was Garret Cagan—the man she had loved; the man she had lost. The man her father had paid to be rid of.

No... It couldn't be.

Her tight dress bit into her ribs, and she felt slightly faint. She swayed forward, but her feet were frozen to the marble floor.

"Is something wrong, Noelle?" Armand whispered.

Her throat was as dry as dust. "A glass of water... anything," she rasped.

She hardly noticed when Armand pressed her arm and then vanished. Her entire attention was on the other man.

"Garret..." She whispered his name aloud, this time with certainty.

He was no longer the gentle, unsure young boy she'd loved when she'd been an untried girl, but a man, almost a stranger, a man who was harder and tougher than any she had ever known. As she stared into his harsh, set face, she knew that all he saw was a frivolous and terribly silly little flirt. She went rigid.

It had been seven years since she'd seen him. Seven years since she'd been sent away to forget him and to finish her schooling—first to a private high school and then to college. Seven years since he'd been paid off. Five years since *Grand-mère* had told her triumphantly that he'd married.

Grand-mère had also told her when he'd had a child. But it was Mama who had told Noelle that his wife had been killed and that he'd been paralyzed with guilt ever since the tragedy.

What was he doing here tonight? There could be only one answer—he had to be one of the plainclothes detectives. But why would he work for the Martins—if only for a night—when she knew he hated them for paying him off and kicking him out?

She realized she should stop looking at Garret, but his dark gaze trapped her and made her feel she was a doe at bay and he a predator closing in for the kill. For seven years she had been running from the emotion in her heart that he alone had aroused.

The tuxedo he wore gave him a cultured look, but she wasn't fooled. His elegant attire didn't conceal the power of his heavily muscled body, nor mute the chiseled edges of his sun-darkened features. His face was different from the other guests—harder, not as softly molded as Beaumont's was, and infinitely more dangerous. There was knowledge in Garret's black gaze that told her he understood her, intuitively, in a man-woman way Beaumont never would. Knowledge that told her he remembered those glimmering afternoons of young love as well as their dark nights of passion. Garret could never fit into her staid and proper world, even if he wanted to.

She was a woman now, no longer a young, impressionable girl he could easily seduce. She knew him too thoroughly. There was no way he could threaten her and the future her family wanted for her.

He lifted his champagne glass in her direction in a mock toast. Her self-confidence evaporated. Her heart began to pound rabbit-fast; blood rushed into her cheeks. Although his glass touched his lips, he did not sip from it. But his gesture mobilized her, and for some reason, she lifted her beaded gown and ran blindly from the room, in a flurry of white skirts and fright, down the white marble hall, past glittering, chattering guests, through the tall French doors, out into the icy moonlit darkness of the garden.

Away from Garret, and the danger of all that he could make her remember.

The semitropical vegetation was lush and concealing, but before she could hide, rough callused fingers grabbed her elbow and spun her around. The moment Garret touched her, she began to tremble.

In the cold moonlight, the wedding ring he still wore on his left hand glittered.

Mon Dieu. So it was true. He couldn't get over the death of his wife.

Mon Dieu. In that moment, Noelle knew that she had never gotten over him.

"Scared, *chère?*" Garret smiled, his beautiful white dangerous smile.

She backed away from him until her bare back touched a cold brick pillar. "No. I just needed some air."

His black eyes laughed at her. "Liar. You're breathless."

She managed a stiff smile. "From running."

He chuckled softly. "Because of me, no?"

He came closer, flicked her diamond necklace with his fingertip so that it sparkled in the moonlight. She felt the warmth of that finger in the marrow of her soul.

"I—I can't believe Papa hired you."

"He didn't. I talked a friend into letting me substitute for him. I've been reading about you in the papers. How you waited to come out because you didn't want to be a Carnival queen until your sister came out and was one as well. I wanted to see you again."

His large hands spanned the back of her waist. His fingertips were like fire.

The muscles in her stomach contracted sharply. "You always were...pushy."

He shrugged. "Ambitious. Is that so wrong?"

She remembered her father's cold assessment. "Cagan's a gold digger. Pure and simple. He's on his way up, and I won't have the son of my cook use my daughter as the first rung in his ladder."

"And you always were a shallow little heartbreaking flirt," he said. "Maybe you haven't changed any more than I have."

She looked away into the darkness of the garden so that he could not see how deeply his barb cut her. "Perhaps," she said with feigned lightness, "I flirt with many because I cannot have the only one I ever wanted."

"Tell me," Garret demanded, "did you ever wonder what happened to me...after that night when your father kicked me out for good? Or did you just go merrily on? You probably had a new boyfriend within a week at your fancy school. Vincent, possibly? Like I said, you were always a flirt, yes?"

"No."

"All I know is that I never heard from you again," Garret said coldly.

"You married..."

"Not for two years, *chère*. Not till I knew for sure you were never coming back."

"Why would I come back when Papa told me you took money to stay away from me? He said the only reason—"

"That's a lie!" The grooves on either side of Garret's mouth deepened into an expression of cynicism. "I never took his money. Maybe I was stupid, but I refused."

"Then where did the money for Mannie's come from?"

"It was a secret loan—from your mother to mine—but later. Every penny of which we repaid—with interest."

"But Papa said—"

"Do you think I give a damn what he said? He would have said anything to keep us apart. Ask Bibi, if you don't believe me."

For a long moment, silence stretched between them, a silence that was as thin and tight as her nerves. Garret was the first to look away, his dark face filled with contempt. Suddenly she knew that he was speaking the truth. Just as suddenly she had to know the whole truth.

"So what did happen to you after..." Noelle hesitated.

"After your father found us together and fired both my mother and me on the spot?" His dark eyes bored holes into her. She could feel them even when she turned away. "It wasn't fun," Garret said with deadly softness. "We were fired by the only employer we'd ever had and given no references. He offered me money, but I thought the price was too high. You see, I had some peculiar southern notion about honor. There was a time when I didn't know if we'd make it."

"*Mon Dieu.* I never thought..."

"No, you were busy flirting, wearing beautiful clothes—"

"I thought I could forget you..."

"I had to quit college. Mama was too sick with shame and worry to hold a job. We went to New Orleans, lived in the lowest tenements. I worked at odd jobs, pumping gas, waiting tables, cooking. Finally I scraped up enough money to finish school and help Mama open the restaurant. It was just a tiny hole-in-the-wall in a bad neighborhood at first. But we developed the reputation for good food. Your mother came by to see my mother and her restaurant, and the two of them worked out a loan. We couldn't hire help.

I had to work at my job and at the restaurant. Then I met Annie. She was sweet. We had Louis. Things got better for a while.... But because of me, that dear angel died." His voice broke, and he shuddered, unable to go on. "Damn. I still can't talk about it." He turned away, not wanting Noelle to see his pain. "Well, I've seen you. You can go back to your damn party."

Through the French windows beneath the dazzle of the chandeliers the guests were waltzing. Beaumont would be looking for her. And Armand. All that seemed another world.

Her world had suddenly become a dangerous, tall, dark man who'd turned his back on her, whose voice and eyes had held nothing but contempt for her. Yet she felt his sorrow as if it were her own. Being with him seemed vitally important. Sharing his pain seemed a natural part of regaining his esteem.

Slowly she went to him, circling his waist with her hands, laying her head gently against his broad back. She felt him tense, but he did not shove her away.

"Garret, I never forgot you, and I was so sorry for you when your wife died." Noelle felt his great body flinch. "You deserved to be happy. I wanted you to be."

"It was because of me, because of my work as a cop that she was killed two years ago."

"No."

"You don't know," he said, his deep voice hoarse, tortured with self-loathing.

"Yes, I do. When I heard about it, I talked to a lot of people. I wanted to go to you, but—"

He whirled around.

Her blood ran cold at the sight of his harsh pain-glazed face. There was pure agony in his eyes, and the most terrible loneliness. But she felt his feelings as if they were hers.

Instinctively she knew that he had locked his grief inside him, that he had sought comfort from no one.

And she knew what that was like—losing someone you desperately wanted, not being able to cope alone, having no one to help you. Hadn't she once been a lonely girl, sent away to boarding school because she loved the wrong man? How many lonely nights had she cried herself to sleep? How many lonely nights had there been no one to hold her, to comfort her, to feel sorry for her loss? Then she had learned that he had married. Yes, she had flirted. Yes, there had been many light, casual, chaste relationships—friendships really—with men. But never once had her heart been involved.

Without thinking she blindly flung herself into his arms. For a moment he was stiff, unyielding, but slowly her gentleness won him to her purpose. Her fingers touched his cheek, softly, caressingly. Their bodies remembered things that their minds had commanded them to forget. She cradled his black head against her own, rocking him, stroking his hair, crooning to him.

"It wasn't your fault. No matter what you think. You've got to go on. I'm glad you came tonight. I'm sorry for what Papa and *Grand-mère* did to you. I've wanted to see you again for years and years."

"You knew where to find me."

"But . . ."

"It doesn't matter," he said at last. "Maybe I didn't want to believe in you."

He began to talk. At first she could make out nothing from the incoherent jumble of words that he muttered swiftly in a hoarse undertone. Then she caught the drift of what he was saying. He spoke of Louis, his only child, who'd seen Annie murdered. Louis wouldn't talk. He was four and falling behind children his own age. Garret didn't know what to do.

After a long time, Garret became calmer. He let her go. "I don't usually push my troubles on people. Especially not—"

"I know."

"Look—"

"It's okay," she whispered.

"You'd better get back."

She clung to him. She never, never wanted to go back. Her glittery world seemed shallow and unappealing.

Suddenly a tall blond man came to the door and looked out into the garden. Beaumont stepped onto the terrace and called her name. "Noelle."

Noelle shrank more deeply into the shadows, pulling Garret with her, holding on to him tightly, and sealing his lips with a fingertip.

Garret's expression lost some of its grimness. Beaumont yelled again, and when Noelle ignored him, Garret smiled at her conspiratorially.

At last Beaumont gave up and went inside.

"Vincent hasn't changed."

"No."

"You're still leading him a merry chase, as well as every other eligible bachelor in the parish."

She savored the thrill of Garret's hard body molded against hers. "Because I don't want to be caught—by any of them."

Seconds passed by in a taut silence. "At least not yet," Garret said in a low, cynical tone.

"Not tonight," she agreed. She held Garret fiercely. "Not now."

His black eyes studied her. "What does that mean?"

"It means I want to play hide-and-seek with you."

Releasing her abruptly, he stepped away.

She remembered sunlit afternoons in a garden with green, shimmering leaves. She had run away from the house, from Beau and Eva to find Garret. Noelle had chased him shamelessly, darting from behind pale columns, hidden from him, been found by him, been held breathlessly close against his male body for tingling moments before he released her. Beau had screamed from the veranda for her to come back, but he was too terrified of snakes to follow her.

"That's the game that started all the trouble," Garret murmured dryly.

"If you call it trouble."

He laughed softly. "I do."

She felt even more magically attracted to him than she had as a girl. He was still every bit as dangerous, every bit as forbidden.

This was not a casual flirtation—casually indulged in, casually abandoned.

"Do you have a car?" she whispered.

"What?"

"I don't feel like small talk. I want you to take me away. Somewhere . . . less complicated . . . than all this."

"If I take you anywhere, things will become infinitely more complicated."

"I don't care."

"What about your family?"

"They don't have to know."

"Hide-and-seek?" His dark eyes blazed.

She put her hand in his. After a long moment his long brown fingers closed over it.

* * *

In his truck he used his radio to call in and request a replacement for his job at the Martin party. Then they were speeding down Prytania Street, past Audobon Park.

"Where are we going?" she asked as the truck raced along the freeway toward the lake.

"Sailing. I have a boat. Sometimes when I stay in the city at night, I sleep on it."

The comment was provocative. It hung in the thick, silent warmth in the truck.

They didn't sail, at least not that night. They went to his boat and changed clothes, taking turns using the tiny cabin. She never asked who the jeans and blouse he got for her from his locker belonged to. She was too glad to be rid of the confining gown.

After they changed, he took her to Mannie's on the lakeshore. Before they ate, he led her back to the kitchen where Mannie was dashing around inspecting trays of food while she lifted the lid of steaming pots of crabs and crawfish.

Suddenly one of the cook's skillets began to smoke. Mannie dashed to it. "Anytime you see some smoke coming from your roux, throw it out, or you be sorry. A burned roux looks good, and the bad cook, she'll try to sneak it by, but it just spoil her crab and her fish."

"Look who I brought, Mama."

Mannie put the skillet down and hugged Noelle affectionately. "I missed you, *chère*. We had some hard times, yes. But the good times, they come back. I'm fatter, yes?"

The roll around her waist was rounder.

"No."

"You sweet liar, *chère*." Mannie turned to her son. "She's too skinny. You two stay and eat, yes?"

Despite the line waiting for tables, Mannie led Noelle and Garret to a table by a window with a view of the lake. Above them a ceiling fan turned lazily while Garret drank a beer and had gumbo. Noelle had a bowl of bouillabaisse and garlic toast. Somebody kept putting quarters into the jukebox, playing blues music. The meal was wonderful. It reminded Noelle of her childhood when Mannie had been the Martin cook.

While they ate, Noelle and Garret talked. About everything—politics, books, sailing, antiques, law enforcement—everything except themselves. But they intuitively knew there would be time for that.

At last he said, "You're everything your family wanted you to be when they broke us up and sent you away to those fancy schools. You're beautiful, cultured—a social star. You even run your mama's business."

"Yes." At that moment she was wondering if she'd ever really cared about any of it.

"And I'm a cop. A detective. A good one. And proud of it." He smiled ruefully. "Or at least I was until Annie died. But even though I'm not the poor boy I was then, your father and grandmother wouldn't want us to have a relationship any more now than they did back then."

Noelle and Garret were enveloped with the husky sound of a saxophone playing the blues.

Her gaze locked on his, and his black eyes took her back to that brief, idyllic summer when they'd realized they were in love, when they'd been cruelly separated by her family. Her attachment to him had been much more than a mere flimsy, adolescent infatuation. She'd never forgotten him. And suddenly she realized that all the years in between had lacked that special luster he alone had given her. She felt it again, every time she looked at him. It was almost as if they'd never been apart. Her heart pounded harder. The moon was more brilliant, the night darker, the air sweeter, the food more succulent and richly spiced. The blues sound was more melancholy. Time seemed to be rushing past in a kaleidoscope of deeply felt emotions.

"For years after they sent you away and threw me out I told myself I hated you," he said. "I imagined you going to that fancy school as rich and privileged as ever while I was starving in the street."

"I wasn't all that happy." She glanced impishly at the mountain of crab shells and shrimp tails on his plate. "And you certainly don't look like you're starving."

He laughed. Then he ordered café au lait and *beignets*.

"You're trying to get me fat," she whispered.

He just grinned at her.

When they finished eating, he grabbed her hand, turned it over in his. "I still want you, Noelle, more than I should, but the differences between us are greater than ever. If you're smart you'll ask me to take you back to your party."

His eyes were warm. Every time she looked at him it was as though his eyes touched her and her body was set aflame.

"I'd rather go sailing," she managed in a throaty voice that didn't sound like hers.

He flashed her a searching look. "Tonight? Alone? With me?"

She nodded.

"It's a cold night," he said.

"We don't have to sail...."

He gripped her hand and then released it fiercely. He knew what she really wanted. Without another word, he left a tip and led her outside.

When they reached his boat, he grabbed a line, pulled the sloop over and helped her on board. Then he jumped from the dock to the boat. The boat rocked gently, and Noelle fell against him.

"Easy, *chère . . .*"

"I don't know starboard from port."

"Tonight you won't need to know."

Then his lips were on hers, harder, hotter, more urgent than she remembered, his hands moving down her body, and she forgot everything except the exquisite pleasure that was happening to her.

He let her go, but he was breathing as hard as she was as he unlocked the hatch. She climbed clumsily down the stairs.

The cabin was dark and close. There was a vague mustiness in the cool air. She thought it the most divinely cozy place in all the world. Above them the sky was dark velvet twinkling with diamond-bright stars.

She fell against something, and he took her in his arms again and guided her to the bunk. She stared into his eyes, her heart racing.

She drew a quick, shallow breath.

He yanked at something on his left hand, opened a drawer. There was the clink of a metallic object rolling across the bottom of the drawer.

There was no more talk. He touched her hair, twining his fingers in the long red flames, brushing it away from her neck so that he could kiss her. She felt the rasp of his tongue against her cool skin, and a burning sensation began to build in the center of her being. She touched his hand and realized he'd taken off his wedding ring.

Time had stopped and there was nothing but the two of them. The night belonged only to them.

She closed her eyes and let it begin. And the darkness became passion and the passion, swirling darkness. It was as if all the years in between had never been.

Afterward he wanted her again immediately. "I thought once would be enough," he murmured as he pulled her down on top of him.

She only laughed huskily, urgently.

They made love until dawn, until the sun was flame in a purple sky, and their love was even wilder and more exciting than it had been when they were kids. Years of loneliness and need and heartbreak were all mixed up with the passion. Each time was an explosion of deep, primitive longing.

Noelle felt alive, so alive every cell in her body seemed to tingle. She knew that *Grand-mère* and Papa would say it was wrong, that Garret was wrong. They would say what they had said before—that she should marry a rich man with impeccable social standing because that was the only kind of man she could trust to marry her for herself alone. She knew what they thought of Garret, of his humble beginnings, of his ruthless ambition. She had been raised to believe she should lead a different sort of life than he led. She didn't want to hurt her family again, but she didn't want to hear anything against Garret, either. It seemed to her that for as long as she could remember he had been a part of her, a part she'd been taught to deny. Every flirtation with every other man had been a vain attempt to run away from her need for this one man. It was as if there were some mystical bonding between them, and all the years of separation and misunderstanding had never occurred.

But she didn't want to make her family unhappy again. And so she decided to keep this precious, private thing a secret, at least for a while. It was an old habit, keeping important parts of herself locked away.

She would be the dutiful daughter by day.

And Garret Cagan's woman by night.

She would have the best of both worlds until the right time to make her decision came along. If she was careful, what could possibly go wrong? Who would be hurt?

How could she have forgotten that when two worlds collide, both worlds shatter?

The dogwood blossoms that Noelle was holding came back into focus. A single tear splashed from her cheek onto an ivory petal that already seemed to be wilting.

Mon Dieu.

Everything had gone wrong. Passion had exploded into tragedy. Everyone had been hurt.

She remembered that last horrible night when she'd nearly died, when she'd lost the baby, when *Grand-mère* had had her stroke and lain as pale as death, unable even to speak. When she herself had recovered, Noelle had knelt at her grandmother's bedside and had made a promise that she never intended to break again.

Noelle remembered the two long years in Australia— years of guilt and denial, clouded by fresh adventure and a tragedy that had prevented her return to Louisiana.

Looking up from the flowers, through the blur of tears, she saw that a faint breeze was stirring the moss draperies and causing ripples on the bayou. A pair of ducks paddled by in the lush, glimmering silence.

Noelle took the flowers and walked slowly back to the house, then up to her bedroom where she shut the door, pulled her purse out of a drawer and fumbled for her airline tickets to Europe.

Downstairs she could hear the others laughing and talking. Someone had put on a record of Christmas carols. She scarcely heard the music.

She thought of Louis, growing up like an orphan with his grandmother; Louis, locked in his world of silence as

Grand-mère had been. She thought of Garret and his stubborn loneliness, but Garret wouldn't let her try to help Louis. He didn't really want her to be a part of his child's life. Nor was there a place for Garret in her own life.

Slowly she skimmed the pages of her tickets. Then she put them down. She went to the mirror and saw that her hair had come down when she'd run in the garden. Carefully she repinned it into the chignon from which it had fallen, pinning it tightly so that not a single hair escaped.

She shoved a final pin into her hair and winced from the pain of it digging into her scalp. The sophisticated, backswept hairdo gave her the regal look of a great lady.

There was only one decision she could make.

Studying her coldly beautiful reflection in the mirror, she sank to the bed, her posture as still and correct as a marble statue's. Her skin had never looked whiter, nor her hair redder, or her golden eyes more luminously desolate.

It was a dear battle that she fought with her heart. It would cost her much. No one would ever know how much. Not even Garret.

Only geographical distance could safeguard her from the temptation of Garret's embrace, from the temptation of going to Louis despite Garret's wishes.

She had to go away and stay away until time erased all memory of Garret and his little boy, until her wild and impetuous nature was safely contained. Because she couldn't safely marry Beau or anyone else until she did.

Tomorrow she would fly to Europe with Eva and concentrate on antiques. That would mean that she would miss Carnival, and she had already received invitations to more than a dozen balls. Beau would be upset when she did not come back.

She let herself imagine Garret one last time—storming into her antique shop, sacrificing his own job to keep her safe. Again she saw him loping toward her at the airport, a lonely tense figure. She remembered her own leap of excitement when she'd seen him; the way passion had flamed in his eyes when he'd begged her to come back to him. How kindly he'd treated her grandmother.

Long ago one shimmery spring afternoon when Noelle had hardly been more than a child she'd first lain with Garret on a bed of violets and given herself—body and soul—to him forever.

No....

Eva placed the receiver gently into Noelle's numb fingers. "It's Detective Cagan. For you."

"Tell him...please...that I can't talk to him," Noelle begged.

"But he swore it was an emergency. He's not the sort of man to take no for an answer."

Noelle shuddered delicately. "H-hello."

"Merry Christmas, *chère*." Garret's voice was a husky caress, but it jarred through Noelle's nervous system. "Did you get my present?"

"Y-yes. It's...beautiful."

"Are you wearing it?"

"No," she whispered in a quiet but emphatic voice.

"That's too bad, *chère*. You have the most beautiful throat...and shoulders...and—"

"Stop!"

He laughed raspily.

Eva was slipping gracefully out of the door, closing it softly behind her.

The plastic receiver was as cold as ice in Noelle's shaking fingers. She felt compelled to tell him—immediately.

"I—I decided that I'm not coming back to New Orleans. I'm flying directly to Europe from Baton Rouge," she blurted out on a breathless note.

"That's bad news, *chère*," he murmured. "Very bad. I was looking forward to seeing you—and soon. The reason I called was that I've got good news, yes."

Something in his smooth, deeply melodious, very-French tone gave her a doomed feeling. "I don't understand," she whispered faintly.

"I've caught your bank robber, *chère*."

"What?"

"You were right about him. Marc Fontaineau's really just a poor kid who made a stupid mistake because he was so desperate he couldn't think straight. He didn't actually attack Eva. She got scared and fell down. That bank did foreclose on him. I talked to the president of the bank, and he's determined to take the kid's mother's house and send the kid to the pen. The house is sitting on a valuable corner near a freeway. But in thirty days mother and son will both be out in the street—homeless—if someone doesn't do something fast. His mother's sick. That's why she can't work and pay the note. If Marc's in the pen, which he will be because the bank president wants to throw the book at him . . ."

In the hushed stillness of the bedroom Noelle clung to the phone as if to a lifeline.

"Garret, you can't do that! He's just a boy. You know better than anyone what it's like to be poor and struggling like that. You have to do something. You can't just leave him there."

"Me? You were the one so all-fire determined to help this kid. Not me. I nearly lost my job because of him."

"Garret!"

"Ouch! My ear! Don't shout so loud, *chère*."

"Damn your ear, you low-down Cajun snake!" But she spoke in a whisper.

"Careful, *chère*. Remember, you're talking to an officer of the law." This was said in a holier-than-thou purr.

"What do you want? Why did you call?"

"I told you before you left. I want you to come back to me. The kid needs you. He could go to prison for a lot of years. Where he's going, up river, they never even heard of the concept of rehabilitation."

Any man who could live apart from his own lonely son could certainly send another boy to the pen without a second thought.

"I could help you, *chère*. And him. Or I could hurt you—both."

"This is blackmail!"

"Don't call it that, *chère*, no." Garret almost sounded genuinely hurt. "I just wanted to wish you a Merry Christmas and to let you know what's been going on. To see if you liked my present. I've been lonelier than hell."

She slammed the phone down and hoped fervently that the sound deafened him.

She wasn't going back to New Orleans.

She wasn't!

Her hand went to her pocket and she pulled the velvet box out. A hot fire was burning inside her, consuming her, until her rage blotted out the tenderness his gift had originally inspired. The room was still and silent. Downstairs she heard Beau laughing. Already he conducted himself as a future in-law.

She had to do something or go crazy. So she threw the box with all her might across the room. Her aim was off, and it barely cleared her bed. It didn't clear her nightstand. Instead it smashed into her little porcelain clock with gold cherubs, a favorite piece she'd treasured since childhood.

She lunged to save it, but the clock fell, shattering into a thousand pieces. She sank beside it, more furious than before, blaming Garret for everything, most especially for her clock.

Eight

"She what?" Garret exploded.

It took only one stunned second for his blood to come to a boil.

He pivoted back in his chair, yanked the knot of his tie loose and ripped open the top button of his shirt.

Johnson was silent, an ominous presence in the tiny office. On Garret's desk was Marc Fontaineau's police report. Garret had been going over it when Johnson had crept stealthily into his office and shut the door.

"I said Miss Martin, the one with the red hair—"

"Dammit. I know which one. Why didn't you stop her before she got to him?"

"I didn't recognize her until she was on her way out and took her scarf off her hair and winked at me. She told the guard she was Fontaineau's sister, so he let her in to see the kid. She was with him about ten minutes. Now the kid won't open his mouth. I thought we were on the verge of making a deal.''

"No doubt she thinks she's helping him." Garret hesitated, picked up a pencil and Fontaineau's police report and thumbed through the pages. "Johnson, I'll handle this from here."

But Johnson didn't budge.

Garret glanced up, his dark gaze glittering with anger. "Well?"

"Sir, there's something else."

"What?"

"She posted Fontaineau's bail. He's out—as free as a bird.''

"And so desperate he may do something else if I don't get to him fast. What is she trying to do to me?"

"Maybe she's showing you who's really the boss."

Not by the flicker of an eyelash did Johnson reveal how immensely he was enjoying himself at Garret's expense.

But Garret knew. He broke the pencil he was holding. "I thought I told you to get the hell out of here."

"Now is that any way to talk to a fellow officer of the law?"

"Hey, I'm not in the mood—"

"So I see." Johnson leaned down and picked up a half of the broken pencil. The corners of his mouth had begun to twitch, but he fought valiantly to suppress his smile.

When he kept smirking beside the desk, Garret got up, went to the door and held it open for him.

Reluctantly Johnson slowly shuffled out of the room.

Alone once more, tension rippled through Garret. He picked up the police report. His gaze was hard and black as he scanned it once more before he tossed it impatiently back to his desk. He might as well shred the thing. Noelle Martin was running this case, not him.

Noelle had been back in New Orleans a week, and what had she done? At every point she'd defied him. And now this. If he didn't take her in hand, soon all his men would be secretly laughing at him behind his back. Not just Johnson.

A week ago Garret had forced her to come down to the station to pick the Fontaineau kid out of a lineup. Instead she'd sulkily viewed the lineup, taken one look at Fontaineau's blond head and said that none of the people looked familiar.

"The next thing you'll tell me, *chère*," Garret had said, "was that Fontaineau just dropped by your mother's shop and talked you into closing early so the two of you could have a friendly chat about whether or not he should give the money back to the bank."

"Why, Garret, you're so clever." She'd batted her eyes then, like a Southern belle—just to mock him. "Why, that's exactly what happened."

Garret had even yelled at her, but nothing he'd done or threatened had done a lick of good. Afterward she'd been coldly furious at Garret because she hadn't wanted to come back to New Orleans. Garret had been equally furious—so angry that when he'd driven her home to the high-rise apartment on St. Charles Avenue with the view of the river that she'd just leased, he hadn't dared go up for fear he'd throttle her.

Garret picked up the phone and dialed her at work. On the sixth ring he glanced at his watch and realized how late it was.

He dialed her home number.

"Hello." Noelle's voice was silky and vibrant.

The sound of it evoked an immediate electric response in him. Then he realized she must have been expecting someone else. Vincent? At the thought, a muscle in Garret's stomach pulled.

"It's me—Garret," he muttered in a fierce, low tone.

There was a hush on the other end. He almost expected her to slam the phone down.

"I hear you came by the station this morning," he whispered.

"So? Is there a law against it?"

Her tone was light, sarcastic, but he caught an edge of fear in it.

"Against what you did—yes. I'm coming over."

"To arrest me?" Again, that light sarcastic tone angered him.

It was time he shook her up a bit. "I've got a better idea, *chère*," he murmured suggestively.

"Garret—no!"

"We've got a lot to talk about," he said grimly.

"Not tonight. Tomorrow. Any other time."

"Tonight, *chère*!"

"I've got a date with Beau. It's important."

"So is this," Garret ground out, fighting to control his temper.

"Garret, please—"

"Cancel it."

"No."

For a long moment neither of them said anything. Then she banged the phone down.

His office was silent except for the dial tone hissing like an electronic serpent in his ear. He could feel the heat rushing into his face as new fury exploded inside him. No one could make him madder than Noelle. No one. He hated the way she thought it was her God-given right to treat him arrogantly—as if he were still some underling she used from time to time because she found him amusing. He felt like hurling the phone across the room. Instead, with a shaking hand, he replaced it gently on the cradle.

It was time he started calling the shots.

He ripped his coat off the back of his chair and raced out of his office.

Garret braked his truck to a stop in front of the fire hydrant at the corner of Noelle's apartment building. He was about to jump out when he remembered how critical Noelle always was of his appearance. He leaned over and studied himself hurriedly in the rearview mirror.

Damn, he was a wreck. Vincent had probably been born in a three-piece, flawlessly cut suit with his hair neatly slicked back on either side of that permanent part.

With deft, impatient movements, Garret quickly buttoned his collar and tightened the knot of his tie. He ran a comb through his hair, but a thick unruly lock tumbled back across his brow almost at once.

As he hopped out of his truck with a large brown sack in his hand the doorman came rushing toward him. "Hey, mister, are you blind? You can't park there! This is a fire lane!"

With casual arrogance Garret tossed the doorman his keys. "Move it if you need to." Then Garret yanked his wallet out of his hip pocket and flashed his badge. "I'm here to see Miss Martin," he whispered conspiratorially.

The doorman's face registered disbelief, then shock. "Miss Martin—the police?"

"She's not in too much trouble, but keep it under your hat," Garret commanded crisply. "And another thing, if a Mr. Beaumont Vincent should turn up for Miss Martin, keep him down here till I get through. This is a private matter."

The doorman nodded gravely. Garret hurried past him into the lobby toward the elevators before the delectable aroma of Mannie's fried oysters and onion rings wafting from the brown bag aroused the doorman's suspicions....

The plush ninth-floor hall was deserted when Garret stepped out of the elevator. He rang Noelle's doorbell.

He heard her bare toes padding eagerly across the carpet. "I'm not quite ready, Beau—" There was a lilt in her voice—a lilt Garret didn't like because it was for Beau.

When she cracked the door, Garret pushed it open. In the next second, he shoved her gently back and slammed the door behind him. He shot the bolt of the dead lock.

"You!" she gasped, her golden eyes ablaze. "You have no right to barge in here uninvited."

Vaguely he was aware of spacious, whitewashed, sky-lighted rooms, of extravagant tapestries on the walls, of wonderful old things from different periods cleverly displayed in their high-rise setting.

"I told you I was coming, *chère*," he murmured softly.

"I don't want you here."

He scarcely noted the fury in her low tone. His own emotions were blazing out of control.

All he saw was woman—*his* woman.

Dammit! She was wearing next to nothing! And for Beau!

Her fiery hair was still moist from her shower. Silken strands of it were glued sexily against her neck. Thin pink silk in the form of a wraparound robe sashed at her waist clung to her slightly wet female shape. He could see the outline of each nipple pushing against soft damp silk. He caught the scent of wild roses, and every cell in his hard male body reacted.

"I told you, Garret Cagan, I have a date," she stated imperiously.

She kept backing away from him as he followed her soundlessly into the room.

He set the sack of oyster poor-boy sandwiches and onion rings on the table.

"I know—with me."

"With Beau," she corrected.

"Is that how you dress for him? Or undress for him?" Garret demanded, jealous.

She went white, and her pale, distraught face touched him more than he wanted it to. Dear God, she was so beautiful and so vulnerable looking, never more so than now with that glazed look of pain in her eyes.

His emotions were at war. He wanted to comfort her tenderly. He wanted to seize her, to crush her soft shape against his hot body, to carry her into the bedroom, to make her accept him until he drove all thoughts of Vincent or any other man from her mind and heart.

"Beau is a gentleman. He would never..."

Garret's lips curved in a bitter smile. "Act like me."

"Exactly," she replied. "And if you think you can run my life like you own me, Garret Cagan, you're—"

"Right," he finished silkily. "When you came back to New Orleans, you came back to me."

"No."

"Maybe you didn't realize that was what you were doing, *chère*," he drawled lazily.

She flushed. Her eyes were wild as she glanced from him to her open bedroom door. Suddenly she made a desperate dash for freedom toward that room. In a single lunge he caught her, pulling her just inside the door, seizing her by the wrists and hauling her effortlessly against his chest. Her long legs fit against his, and he felt on fire with the slim sweep of her body against his own.

During the struggle, her sash came unknotted and fell to the floor. Her robe gaped open, and he saw that she wore nothing but a lace bra and panties.

Hungrily his eyes slid over her. His heart began to pound violently at the sight of the transparent pink lace cups that contained her breasts, at the filmy bikini panties that revealed more than they concealed. Desire flooded through him, but he fought it. And the effort made him shake.

He held her fast, adjusting the position of her arms behind her back, so that he could span both her wrists with one hand, leaving his other free.

He could feel her quivering. He did not know whether with revulsion or anticipation. All he knew was that he could feel her skin burning with the same heat as his own. He had to show her that in his own way he worshiped her more reverently than any gentleman ever could—especially more than her thin-blooded Beau.

With his free hand Garret smoothed the wild red tangles away from her face. Then he caressed her cheek. His fingers trailed lower, exploring her gently until she lay her head back against the wall and sighed softly in a long breathless shudder of defeat. His fingertips slid down her belly and lower.

A flush burned across her cheeks; her eyes were dark with desire. Her pulse thudded in unison with his. Neither of them knew the exact moment when she had lost the will to fight him, but both of them knew she had. He nuzzled his cheek against the softness of her thick hair and lightly pressed his lips against her forehead.

"Noelle, *chère*..." he murmured hoarsely.

He had released her wrists, and she was holding on to him, clinging to him fiercely. He felt the touch of her fingers moving the length of his spine.

He was the one who pulled away. She looked wonderingly up at him, expectant, tamed.

His own gaze was cynical as he tilted her face up to him and stared deeply into her eyes. "Don't ever tell me again that you didn't come back to me, *chère*, because I won't believe you. I'm in your blood, a part of you. Maybe you don't like it any more than I do, but you belong to me. You always have. You always will."

Noelle stared back at him, shaking her head as if to deny it, but he could see she was shocked to realize he was speaking the truth. Her pink mouth trembled.

Then he brushed two dangling red curls from her eyes as she struggled to accept this new idea.

"I—I don't know what to do," she said wearily at last. "All I know is that in the past everything has always gone wrong between us."

He shrugged in that gesture of his that was peculiarly French. "Why don't you start by getting dressed?"

"But?"

"Beau's coming over. Remember, *chère*? You and I need to talk. And I brought supper."

"What?" She was smoothing her hair, trying in vain to restore it to order.

"Oyster poor boys—cooked by Mannie herself."

"My favorite."

His voice was low and filled with innuendo. "Why do you think I brought them? There's nothing I like better...than tempting you."

The broad brown crescent river snaked through a New Orleans that gleamed pink in the setting sun. Garret drank his icy beer with a feeling of pleasant expectation as he studied the big freighter inching its way up river. He felt a wave of satisfaction as he remembered how quickly he'd had Noelle melting in his arms as thoroughly caught up by desire as he.

It was too bad he'd had to stop because Vincent was on his way over, but Garret was philosophical. He'd been in a hurry to get over here and settle things between Noelle and himself. But first he had to set Vincent straight. After that there was the police business to smooth over. Then Garret would have all the time in the world to court her, and he was determined not to rush Noelle. That was one of the mistakes he'd made in the past. They had hurried into sex before they were really sure of each other. If she hadn't gotten pregnant... If he hadn't followed her to Raoul's that night ... If he could have listened to her and trusted her instead of getting so damned jealous... If he hadn't been so ready to believe her grandmother... Two years ago, Garret had made a lot of mistakes. The last thing he wanted to do was repeat them.

He heard the bedroom door open. The soft swish of a skirt, the scent of wild roses told him Noelle had entered.

He turned. She was dressed in emerald-green silk. Gold and diamonds sparkled at her throat and ears and hands. She was wearing the necklace he had given her for Christmas. For an instant he studied her wide-spaced slanting eyes, the red fullness of her soft mouth, the slim yet voluptuous figure. He saw the startled golden light in her eyes, the fire in the molten lava of her hair. There was fire in her as well—warmth, desire.

It had been two months since he'd last made love to her. And not one night had passed that he hadn't lain in his bed alone longing for her, longing for the scent and taste of her, for the warmth of her skin next to his after they'd made love and fallen asleep. Every night he'd spent alone his body had been filled with the same tightness, the same aching tension that filled it now.

She came to him. "Enjoying the view?" she asked in a prim, light tone.

He studied the sleek line of her hips, her slim waist, her soft breasts. He felt the fierce need to touch her, to rouse her again.

"Yes," he murmured dryly. "The view is magnificent. You've done wonders with..." With an effort he forced his gaze from her soft voluptuous curves to the furnishings of her apartment. "... with this place. You obviously know how to put things together. I can't even match ties and shirts."

"I know." Demurely she came nearer and touched his tie.

He smiled ruefully. "That bad?"

She nodded, responding to his smile with a rosy blush.

"Then I'll take it off," he murmured.

He unbuttoned his shirt, pulling his tie loose. He unbuttoned another button.

"That's far enough," she whispered huskily.

"So brown throats turn the lady on?" he teased in a low, caressing tone.

"Garret!" But her blush deepened.

He handed her his tie. The tips of his fingers brushed hers. "Just hoping," he said lightly, grinning at her.

Her downcast eyes studied the zillions of black, bumblebee polka dots on the yellow tie. "This is awful. Really awful."

"It caught my eye in the shop."

Her chuckle was warm and vibrant. "I'm sure it did."

"I thought it was colorful."

"Busy," she corrected gently.

"You still haven't taken me shopping."

"You're incorrigible."

He reached out and took her hand, and even that excited him. "That makes us the perfect couple."

Her whiskey-colored eyes were huge. She was so damned pretty every nerve in his body was tingling in sharp awareness of her. Her fingers tightened around his in response.

"Garret, I—" Noelle never finished her sentence.

The telephone began ringing, and she knocked it to the carpet so agitated was she from the warm intimacy of the moment before. She knelt and picked it up. "Why, Beau!" Noelle's eyes flew wide open and then narrowed on Garret as she listened to what Vincent was saying.

Garret decided he'd better escape to the kitchen before she got off the phone. Vincent had begun to yell so loudly that even from the kitchen Garret could hear his every word.

"I said tell your damned doorman to let me come up."

"There's been a mistake, Jean," she whispered a minute later, obviously to her doorman. "Yes, the detective's still up here, but really, he's here on a personal matter. It's perfectly all right for Mr. Vincent to come up."

She hung up just as Garret returned from the kitchen with three place mats and set them on the table.

"What do you think you're doing?" she demanded angrily.

Garret grinned at her. "Setting the table."

"That's not what I meant and you know it. You gave my doorman the impression I was in some kind of trouble with the law. Then you told him—"

"Does Vincent drink milk or water?"

"Don't ignore me!"

The doorbell rang.

"Do you want me to get it or will you?" Garret offered helpfully. "My hands are full."

"I'll get it!" she snapped. "But don't think for a minute I'm finished with you."

"That's good news, *chère*," he murmured softly.

She flung the door open. Beau was a tornado of arrogance and anger as he stormed inside. As always his blond hair was glued to his scalp and his suit flawlessly elegant, but Garret was glad to see his rival looking rattled as hell.

Vincent directed his entire attention to Garret. "What are you doing here?"

"Inviting you to dinner," Garret said with a broad grin as he set a glass of milk down in front of a plate full of oysters.

"Damn! I don't want your soggy oysters. Or milk! I want you out of here."

"Beau!"

"I take it that's a refusal," Garret drawled lazily, picking up the third place mat.

"You're damn right!"

Noelle tried to step between them. "Beau, I understand your anger, but really I must ask you to at least try to be civil."

Garret put his arm around Noelle so tightly she couldn't ward it off. "That's all right, *chère*, you don't have to take my side. I hardly need a backup with a guy like Vincent."

Beaumont turned so purple he looked like he'd swallowed his tongue and was choking on it.

Noelle pushed Garret away and fixed him with a withering glare. "I wasn't defending you, you big blockhead."

"That's the insult you used on me when you were three," Garret said, a pleased nostalgic note in his voice.

"It still fits," she whispered, furious.

Beau walked over to Noelle and daintily used one fingertip to touch the yellow, black-dotted tie she'd forgotten she was still holding. "Just what is this?" He withdrew his finger from the strip of silk with the distaste he might have for a soiled bit of garbage from the gutter.

Garret observed his rival with a self-satisfied grin.

"Oh!" Noelle gasped.

She was about to throw the tie on the table, but Garret caught it in midair and hung it loosely around his neck so that both bright ends dangled against his chest. "Thanks, *chère*." To Beau he said, "Obviously it's a tie—mine. Noelle suggested that I get more comfortable."

Beau was mottled lavender, well on his way to purple again. "Noelle?" he demanded.

"Nothing happened," Noelle said flatly, fixing Garret with a glare.

"Not tonight, no, *chère*," Garret inserted. "Not yet anyway. But maybe Vincent would like to hear about the evening you drove out to my house a couple of months ago, the night you slept all night in my bed."

Beau made a strangling noise in his throat.

Noelle went pink with embarrassment. "Garret, just what do you think you're doing?"

"*Chère*, the man asked a question. He wants to know what's going on between us. I was just letting him know that plenty is. You are mine. I told you—this time we aren't sneaking around."

The silence that fell after this statement vibrated with tension. Vincent hung near the door, outraged, but uncertain what to do next.

Noelle was very pale and shaking with rage.

Garret grinned, pulled out a chair and seated himself at the head of the table as if he were the man of the house. "Well, now that that's settled—supper, anyone?" he offered pleasantly.

"This is too much!" Beau muttered. "Noelle, you may enjoy spending your evenings with this swamp cop from the ghetto, but I don't. I'll be down in the BMW, waiting for you. I'd like to hear your side of this, but if you aren't down in ten minutes, don't bother coming—or calling ever again. I'll consider all our dates to Carnival affairs canceled as well."

Garret punctuated this dramatic ultimatum by crunching into his poor boy. He was chewing vigorously as the door banged shut behind Beau.

"I hope you're happy," Noelle cried, turning on Garret.

He swallowed. "I am. Very." He shot her another wide, white grin.

"Well, I'm going with him."

"Fine," he murmured. With a show of elaborate unconcern, he plucked an onion ring from the sack. "I hope you don't mind if I stay and finish my poor boy. Vincent was wrong about these oysters. They're great. I'll clean up and then lock the place before I go."

"No way. I'm not leaving you alone here."

"Good." He leaped from the table just as she picked up her purse, his supper forgotten, his entire attention focused on the woman.

She stumbled backward, too startled to escape him. "Garret...no...your supper..."

"To hell with my supper. To hell with everything except you, *chère*—you and me."

He gripped her arms and pulled her to him. "I thought that fool was going to stay forever," Garret muttered fiercely, pressing her against his long, hard length. He reached out and caught a handful of shimmering red hair, winding it in his sun-browned fingers, pulling her neck back.

At first she fought him, but he was too engulfed by the searing flame of his own passion to release her. He could feel her trembling under the pressure of his hands as he lowered his mouth and kissed her lips urgently, ravaging their sweetness. She twisted and kicked, but he only kissed her harder, bruising the softness of her lips against his teeth. His mouth trailed down the rigid cord of her neck, kissing her until he became aware of her involuntary shivers every time his mouth touched the hot hollow of her throat.

He heard the harsh intake of her breath with a glow of satisfaction. He licked her throat, and she shivered against his marauding mouth.

"Don't..." she pleaded helplessly even as primitive female instinct had her breasts swelling against green silk.

He ran his tongue the length of her throat again. He felt her arms come up and circle his neck. She wanted him, too....

With a single movement his fingers slid the zipper of her dress open. He pushed it over her shoulders, down her arms, her wrists. She did not fight him. As it pooled at her feet, she stepped out of her shoes in a kind of daze, and he lifted her into his arms.

He was getting in too deep too fast again, just as he always had with her, but he couldn't stop himself. She was burying her face against his throat, kissing him wherever her lips could make contact, shuddering with little moans of ecstasy. He felt her tears of joy against his hot skin.

He held her effortlessly in his arms, and all the time her hands stayed wrapped around his neck as his hard male mouth resumed its ownership of hers. He carried her into her bedroom, to the antique, canopied bed. She lay on the rumple of silken sheets and brocade bedspread, looking up at him as she removed her jewelry, piece by glittering piece. Last of all, she removed the amethyst pendant he had given her. Her eyes were ablaze with sensual need. Quickly he ripped his own clothes off, and tore his watch from his wrist.

She looked like a queen amid the lace pillow shams and silk sheets beneath the carved artistry of the great mahogany bed. For a second the truth of their situation flashed a warning in his mind. She was still the rich society girl— forbidden to a guy from the streets like him, a cop.

He pushed the unwanted thought aside.

Then he was on top of her, and she was twisting and writhing beneath him. He forgot everything that had gone wrong in the past as well as all the future dangers that threatened them. All that mattered was the wild, thrilling glory of having her again.

The world was a mist of red flame devouring them both. And in the middle of the flame was pleasure such as neither of them had ever known before.

He was hard and full when he entered her. She was soft and warm and clinging. He tilted her head back, crushed his lips onto hers, his tongue mating with hers. There was a building wildness in them both, an explosion that seemed to fill the universe.

Afterward he knew that all the years they'd been apart had only sweetened this moment for them both.

"Do you belong to me?" he whispered in the now-dark bedroom.

"I belong to you," she said simply.

He stirred, and rich brocade grazed his skin. His mind was numb. Could she ever really be his?

Then she asked, "But do you belong to me?"

He tensed and lapsed into silence. He became aware of the great bed again, of the silk sheets, of the bedside table where her diamond and gold jewelry lay beside the amethyst pendant he had given her and his inexpensive quartz watch; of the elegant room, of the velvet and gilt of the other restored antiques. Her naked body was soft and pale; she'd never had to do manual labor in her whole life. His body was tough and brown and laced with muscle—because he'd had to use not only his brain but every muscle since the day he'd been born.

The elegant bedroom and the elegant woman belonged to a world he'd only had fleeting glimpses of in the past. His world was peopled by cops and criminals, by cooks and waitresses and the customers who came to Mannie's. All his life he'd worked hard.

He got up and went to the window. With a callused hand he lifted the heavy fold of a brocade curtain aside and stared moodily at the diamond lights of the city sprinkled beneath him. The real world, his world, seemed far away.

It would be so easy to lie and give her the answer she wanted.

But something, some shred of latent honor stopped him.

He was aware of her rolling in the silk sheets, of her body curling itself into a tight ball of lonely misery because of the lengthening silence after her question.

He balled his hands into fists and waited until she cried herself to sleep before he went back to bed.

Nine

The swamp was green and deep and dark—dangerous—a part of her. Here Noelle could wear faded jeans and a cotton shirt and let her hair fall in tangles around her shoulders. Here there were no rules, and she could almost forget who she was.

But not quite.

The swamp's brooding atmosphere mirrored her mood. She was alone and feeling vulnerable as she fished from the stern of Garret's houseboat that was moored in the secret place he and Noelle had loved as children. Garret had bought the houseboat used, and it now served as his fish camp.

"I still come here when I want to get away from it all, *chère*. Only now I've got a roof over my head, a bed and screens to keep the mosquitoes out in the summer," he'd told her as he'd helped her on board earlier that morning, before he'd left her alone while he went to visit Louis.

Noelle understood Garret's love for this particular spot. When they'd been kids they'd often come here in their pirogues and fished. When they'd grown older they'd thrown blankets down on the high ground beneath the cypress trees and picnicked together. In the spring, violets grew thick and lush on every bank. It was here, beneath the swaying gray draperies of moss in the dark shade of the cypress trees, that long ago she and Garret had first made love. It was here that she'd first hoped that they would belong to each other forever.

As Noelle studied the root-laced bayou, it seemed to her that she'd come full circle, back to the beginning of her love for Garret, back to the beginning of all that had gone wrong.

She'd needed this time alone to think because even though this past week seemed a blur of passionate nights, everything was still wrong between them. They were still running from the same inner demons that had always chased them. Even when they were happiest, there was an uneasiness and an uncertainty between them. They came from two worlds. Hers was a life of wealth and the feeling that responsibilities came with that wealth. Garret's life had been tough. He had fought for everything he had, and his identity was equally important to him. He didn't feel he owed anyone an apology for who he was. In the past they'd both hurt each other, and they found it difficult to trust each other.

An approaching pirogue set into motion everything that was alive in the swamp. An unfriendly alligator swatted the water with his tail and then sank beneath a thick patch of water hyacinths. Birds pierced the silence with excruciating protests. Snakes slithered into the impenetrable dark ooze. A turtle jumped off a rotting log into the water.

Noelle glanced up from her fishing line and bobbing cork. Garret stood tall and proud in the narrow boat, his chiseled male profile sharply defined against the muted grays and greens of the swamp as he dug his pole into the soft mud of the bayou bottom. Her throat caught as she looked past him and saw the empty seat in the pirogue. No little boy with shimmering gold hair, only the hard, stubborn man, determined to keep his son to himself.

A tear flickered against her eyelash, but she brushed it away so Garret wouldn't see. Louis had not come. In that moment she realized how much she had hoped that Garret would relent.

Garret poled the pirogue expertly and tied it to the houseboat just as expertly. Robotlike, Noelle helped him.

After he came on board, he pulled her into his arms and buried his mouth along the side of her neck.

"Noelle." He said her name in a raspily caressing tone. "I couldn't wait to get back to you."

For an instant she relaxed against him, seeking comfort in his embrace. Just as quickly, she hated his tenderness.

"Don't," she whispered, frantic to avoid his touch.

He withdrew his lips. His head came back sharply, his gaze narrowed with piercing intensity. Her desolate expression left him in little doubt of what she was feeling.

"So how was Louis?" she asked in a small voice.

"I thought I told—"

"You did. That doesn't mean I'm happy about it."

"Dammit, Noelle, I—" he began.

"Why are you swearing?"

"Because I know what you want."

"But you don't care what I want."

"You know that's not true, no, *chère*," he said in a softer tone. "Didn't I go out of my way to help Marc Fontaineau in spite of your interference? Didn't I advance the Fontaineaus enough cash to make all their back payments due the bank? Didn't I help you get Fontaineau's mother to the hospital so she could have that operation? Didn't I wait with you during the surgery?''

Noelle nodded mulishly. ''Yes.''

''Can I help it if there are still serious charges against Fontaineau?''

''You know I don't blame you for Marc's problems. You've been wonderful—there. It's Louis—''

''Dammit. Why can't our being together again be enough?''

''Because—''

''No.'' Garret's jaw tightened.

''Garret, Mardi Gras is just around the corner. You'll be working very hard then. I'd like to take him to at least one parade.''

''I told you I don't want Louis involved with us! Not yet. He has the painful habit of forming intense attachments to people, especially women. Especially you. When you walked out on him, he couldn't deal with the rejection.''

''Louis needs a mother's love.''

Garret's eyes were as black as death. ''His mother's dead. The last thing he needs is a relationship with you that won't last.''

''I quite agree,'' she answered, taking a deep breath before she turned away.

Everything was blurred by the mist of her tears.

There was a long silence.

''Forget Mardi Gras and taking him to a parade. He's not your child. He's mine!'' Then Garret threw the screen door open so hard that it went flying against the wall. The houseboat shuddered violently.

He stomped inside, and Noelle stayed where she was feeling more lost and desolate than ever. He had gotten rid of Beau, removed her from her own life, and yet he refused to make her a part of his.

She heard Garret light the propane stove, cursing to himself when the matches were too damp and he had to search for another box, swearing again when he burned himself. Later she caught the scent of Cajun spices wafting in the air. Shrimp and crab and frog legs sizzled in a frying pan.

After a while it began to rain gently, but she stayed outside under the shelter of the eaves. Her stomach growled. There was nothing she liked better than Garret's fried shrimp and crab claws and frog legs. But not for the world would she allow him the satisfaction of stumbling mutely in to eat what he'd cooked.

Instead she waited until all was quiet, until he doused the lights and went to bed without her.

Only then did she ease the door open and slip inside where she curled up on the couch and lay tense and awake.

Hours later she was vaguely aware of some sound in the darkness, and then she jumped in fright when something brushed her arm.

It was only Garret touching her. Only Garret's long fingers like tongues of fire on her bare flesh.

"Don't be mad, no, *chère*," he whispered ever so softly.

The breath caught in Noelle's throat. She could feel his tension as he studied her in the darkness.

It was terrible, more terrible than anything, being at odds with him. She had felt again the long, lonely emptiness of the years that she'd been without him. It didn't matter that their relationship wasn't perfect, that his job and his life had made him hard. He was right for her in some way that no one else ever had been. Louis was his son, after all, not hers.

She didn't resist when Garret eased her stubborn, bright head onto his shoulder, when he slipped his arm around her and held her.

She was surrounded by him; his thighs were rock hard, his chest massive and yet warm and comforting. His silence was a comfort, too. For a long time neither said anything more, and gradually she relaxed in his strong arms.

"I'm sorry I pushed you about Louis," she said at last. "I won't do it again."

His hands gently smoothed her hair. "And I'm sorry I said what I did."

But even as he lowered his mouth to hers and the feverish excitement of being with him began to mount, she knew that nothing had been resolved.

The rain storm had passed.

So had their passion. Sex had been a physical act of lust and frustration, not a mating of two minds and souls.

Garret was at the window, gazing out at the mysterious dark poetry of the swamp in the moonlight. He caught that faint odor of damp and rotting vegetation. The wind swirled the wet foliage. The surface of the bayou was alive with ripples.

He turned and became aware that Noelle was awake, too. His thoughts were both tender and troubled as he feasted upon the creamy, silken woman lying in the silvery light, the woman who waited for him to come back to bed and take her in his arms and hold her until they fell asleep.

They were both satiated from their lovemaking, and yet no matter how physically satisfying it had been, something vital had been lacking for both of them. It was as if neither knew how to reach the other. Emotionally, he felt tight and hard, as if he'd had no release at all.

"Come back to bed," she whispered, her voice throbbing.

He wanted to say that their problems couldn't be solved in bed, that he'd tried to solve them there and he'd probably keep on trying.

But he obeyed her, crossing the room in long silent strides, lying down stiffly beside her, refusing to take her in his arms. His mouth was set in a grim line. He shot her a sideways glance. The same lost expression was in her eyes that had been there before he'd made love to her.

"It's not enough, is it?" she asked quietly.

He felt her fingers brush his arm.

"For either of us?" she added.

"No," he admitted, pulling away from her, crossing his arms behind him on his pillow and propping his dark head on top of them.

"Passion never is. We both want everything else—love, trust..."

"Do you blame me, if I can't feel that way about you?" he demanded in a biting, cynical tone.

"Maybe, if you'd just listen to me..."

"You'd better leave Louis out of this."

"Okay. I want to talk about the baby."

"Hell." His voice grew even colder as he remembered the night that had shown him once and forever just how deep the chasm between them really was.

"We have to talk about what happened two years ago, about the night we lost each other. About Raoul. About why I went to his house that evening instead of meeting you at your boat the way I'd promised. About why I couldn't tell you the truth about him."

Garret's head turned on the pillow to stare at her in the darkness. "I know why! For all his faults, a Girouard's social pedigree was infinitely preferable to a Cagan's—even to your grandmother!''

"No!''

Garret muttered a garbled curse. "I never want to think about that night or Girouard again!''

"You've got to listen to me," she pleaded.

"I already feel rotten enough as it is," Garret whispered angrily.

"I wanted your baby," she said, her voice low and gentle, insistent. "More than anything.''

Her words brought a raw ache to his heart. "I don't believe you, *chère*. Your grandmother swore to me you were glad our baby died.''

"*Grand-mère* was out of her mind because I was pregnant by you and unmarried. She was afraid I might be dying. She blamed you for everything, and she wanted to punish you and drive you away.'' Noelle paused. "I wanted to marry you, for us to be together for the rest of our lives and make a home for our child and Louis—despite my family.''

"Then why did you keep our relationship a secret from everyone that mattered to you? You didn't even tell me you were pregnant.''

"Because…because it was so hard for me to face *Grand-mère* and Papa.''

"I wasn't good enough to be the father of your child in their eyes.'' Garret's gaze was hard. "So you went to Raoul…first. Not to me. Did you tell him the baby was his?''

"Raoul loved Eva, you big idiot. Not me!''

"Eva? Do you really expect me to believe—''

"Yes! I knew they were planning to elope secretly. I had to stop them. Since I was pregnant, I had to bring our relationship out in the open. *Grand-mère* hadn't been well.

Whether you believe it or not she has never liked Raoul—despite his . . . social pedigree. She wasn't up to two blows at the same time—my pregnancy plus Eva's elopement with a Girouard. I went to Sweet Seclusion to try to convince Raoul and Eva to wait.''

"Eva and Raoul?'' Garret's gaze flicked sharply to her in disbelief.

"Yes!''

"It's too impossible for me to imagine them together.''

"Don't you remember that he was constantly at Martin House?''

"I thought he was there to see you.''

"Everyone did. I let you think so because I was immature enough to be flattered by your jealousy.''

"Wasn't I jealous enough?'' Garret's mouth thinned. "You were a Mardi Gras queen and always attending all those balls and parties I was excluded from.''

"I thought I could have it all,'' she whispered.

"So . . . Back to that night. When you didn't come to my boat to meet me, I drove out to Martin House to find you. Your car was just leaving when I got there. I followed you to Sweet Seclusion. I figured there must be something between you and Raoul after all, so I drove back to New Orleans. The weather was getting so nasty I couldn't sail, but I went to my boat anyway. I drank a couple of beers, and my anger fed on itself. Then you came, hours after you were supposed to have met me there. I asked you why you were so late, and you didn't even mention your visit to Girouard.''

"When I told you about the baby, you asked . . .''

He sucked in a deep tortured breath. " 'Who's the lucky father?' ''

"I wanted to die," she whispered.

"You nearly did."

"I hardly remember..." He voice was faint.

And yet she did remember—every terrible detail. The houseboat, the lapping of the bayou outside, all the wild swamp sounds, Garret's glittering dark gaze—everything that belonged to the present—blurred.

There was only the mad thudding of her heart. It was two years before. The night was as black as ink, the wind fierce and wet and howling as it swept across Lake Pontchartrain and lashed the hull of Garret's sailboat. The halyards were clanging against the mast. She and Garret were alone inside his airless cabin with the hatch tightly latched and the silence inside seemed to smolder. Occasionally, violent gusts made the boat heel to one side, and she had to grab on to the varnished ladder in the companionway to steady herself.

Noelle was worried about having made Eva and Raoul put their relationship on hold. She was worried, too, about breaking the news of her pregnancy to Garret when he was behaving so strangely tonight, as if something terrible had happened to him, something he wasn't able to confide to her. Garret was so pale that only his dark eyes seemed to be alive—great burning black holes in his drawn face. Not once had his expression softened when he'd lifted his morose gaze from the table and focused it on her. His fingers were locked around the neck of his beer bottle as if it were the handle of a knife. He made the bottle rock back and forth, and the motion was both hypnotic and maddening. He hadn't touched her, hadn't kissed her. He kept watching that incessantly moving bottle, and his remote mood filled her own heart with the desperate desire to scream, to do anything to break the tension.

This isn't the right time to tell him, some inner voice informed her.

Yet the terror of not knowing what was wrong with him made her blurt out her news. "Garret, I'm pregnant."

She wanted him to put his arms around her, to say he was happy. She longed for any sign of happiness.

Instead, her words merely intensified the dark brooding quality of his mood. His expression tensed, and he cocked his head at a funny angle so that she could see the mad pulsing of a corded vein in his neck. But the bottle continued to rock back and forth on the table.

"Who's the lucky father?" His voice was strangled, but he kept moving that bottle.

"Y-you know you are—"

"Do I?" He looked up and began to laugh, but his eyes blazed with emotion.

She flinched with hurt. "You know..."

He was no longer looking at her. His gaze was focused on the cruelly glinting bottle in his fist.

In a haze of agony she realized it was no use trying to talk to him. Something was dreadfully wrong.

Blindly, she turned away. She reached for the hatch, slid it open and rain poured into the cabin. He called her name. She heard only his rage followed by the violent shattering of glass—the beer bottle—he'd either thrown it or dropped it. She struggled up the ladder, desperate to escape him.

He rushed after her into the cockpit. The boat was pitching wildly from the wind. She could barely stand on the slippery deck. All she knew was that she had to get away. She wanted to die of shame, of desolation.

She reached for the dockline. Just as she was pulling the boat nearer to the dock, a gust of wind screamed across the lake.

"Noelle..." Garret lunged to help her, but she twisted away, trying to jump to the dock.

She almost made it. For an instant she tottered in her rubber-soled canvas shoes on the wet wooden planks, but she couldn't get her balance. With a helpless cry, she fell backward into the black icy waters, her skull striking the massive chrome winch on the deck of Garret's boat.

Barely conscious from that blow, gasping with shock from the cold water, she struggled to swim despite the weight of her sodden clothes. A terrible, final, hopeless exhaustion was draining the last ounce of her strength, and she felt herself sinking in a swirl of pain and horror. She wanted to go to sleep, to float peacefully away, to forget about Garret... and the baby. But she couldn't forget her baby. She had to stay conscious. So she fought to swim back toward the boat, to Garret's outstretched hand, but her legs were so numb she could barely kick them.

She closed her eyes. He screamed her name. But the cold murky waters were sucking her under and sweeping her away. She opened her eyes one last time. The last thing she saw was Garret's face, white and wild, his eyes desperate with fear—right before he jumped in after her.

By the time he got to her she was half-drowned. He had raced her to the hospital, and the whole way she'd been too ill to even know he was there. She'd been icy with shock, as still as death. She had wanted him, cried for him soundlessly, but she'd never realized he was there....

A cool breeze stirred the bayou, as well as the draperies of Spanish moss that shrouded the cypress trees. As Garret lay in bed beside Noelle in the houseboat, the bitter memories wouldn't stop for him, either. He remembered holding Noelle's cold lifeless hand in the ambulance as she lay on the stretcher. He kept seeing her white face when he'd asked her who the father was. He'd kept imagining her with Raoul, wondering why she'd gone to him that night before she'd come to him. More than anything he'd wanted to take back his awful words.

No one had ever told her he was there. Her grandmother had had her stroke that same night. He knew now that Noelle had blamed herself for that. As soon as Marlea was better, Noelle had gone away to Australia. Raoul had gone to Africa to fight in some war, and no one in the parish, not even Eva, had heard from him again. No one knew if he was dead or alive. According to local gossip, a check for the maintenance of Sweet Seclusion still came monthly from a Swiss bank account. There were those who said that Eva Martin had never gotten over him.

Garret stared across the tangle of sheets at Noelle. She'd been silent for a long time, and he wondered what she'd been thinking. She was beautiful with her nude, curved body half exposed by the white folds of cotton sheets. Hell. It was best to bury the past.

In a single fluid motion, Garret rolled over and eliminated the distance that separated them. His finger lifted the delicate pendant from her throat and watched it sparkle in the moonlight. He let it drop. It was much lovelier against her skin.

His hands spread over her shoulders. Her flesh was like warm satin. She gasped, and he felt the wonder of her sliding closer and pressing her soft curves against his granite length.

"At least we're together, now," he muttered. "The past doesn't really matter so much."

"But are we—really? And for how long?"

"For as long as we want each other."

"No commitment?"

He looked into her luminous eyes. She was beautiful, so beautiful—pale and soft, with her slanting dark-lashed eyes and her red hair framing her lovely face; rich and spoiled. There was an innocence about women like her, a confidence about life that he didn't have. She still believed she could have anything she wanted. He had learned differently. His nerves tightened, and he looked away, into the darkness beyond her.

"So you still can't believe what I said about what happened two years ago?"

He laughed harshly. "I don't know, but you've got to admit I haven't had much luck in the past with commitments out of you. You always run away. I've had to stay behind and fight my own battles. I didn't always do so well. Annie's dead. Louis won't talk.... But, dammit, I've fought. All I know is that I want you now, and you want me. I doubt very much that you and I could ever have a future together." All he let her hear was his anger, not the fear behind his anger that he was right.

She was about to protest, but his fingers grasped her chin and he turned her face to his. "Nothing we say can change what happened." Then he silenced her anguished response with a kiss that thankfully, at least as far as he was concerned, left her too stupefied to argue further.

She was pulling him on top of her and their passion burned again like the most desperate flame.

Two weeks had passed. Noelle hadn't been able to get that night and her pain out of her mind even after they'd returned to New Orleans together. So now it was Carnival, and she'd left the city and Garret to come to Martin House where she could be alone with her thoughts and *Grand-mère*.

Noelle was in the kitchen making tea and coffee, thinking of Garret instead of concentrating on what she was doing. Suddenly the Meissen sugar bowl slipped through her fingers and shattered on the tile floor. Noelle stared at the priceless yellow and white bits of china and wanted to feel horror. It was a shock to realize that she was too upset about the problems of her relationship with Garret to really care at all.

"What was that?" Marlea cried from the veranda.

Although *Grand-mère* was frail, she still had ears like a lynx's.

"Your favorite sugar bowl."

"Come out here, dear. Let Celia clean the kitchen before you do any further damage. You've been as nervous as a cat ever since we left New Orleans."

Noelle stepped out onto the veranda where *Grand-mère*, who was wrapped in a light woolen shawl, sat rocking slowly back and forth as she sipped a steaming cup of chicory-flavored coffee. The sky that enveloped the house and trees was silver bordered with black edges. The wind off the bayou was cool and strong.

"It feels like a storm is brewing," Noelle said.

"What's the matter, *chère*?" Marlea demanded gently. But the tone held command.

Noelle sank into the wicker chair opposite her grandmother and poured herself a cup. Even though she longed to confide in her grandmother and tell her everything, Noelle couldn't.

"Nothing," she whispered. She brought her cup to her lips and sipped silently, watching the sky darken. "If this weather doesn't get better, some of the Carnival parades may be canceled."

Marlea ignored Noelle's attempt to change the subject.

"I may be old, but I've got eyes in my head. I thought you wanted to come to Martin House. You said you wanted to get away from the city during Carnival."

"I did."

Noelle could feel her grandmother's sharp bright eyes studying her. "Is it Beau?"

"No."

"When I was your age I wouldn't have left New Orleans ever during this time of the year."

"Things were different then."

Marlea sighed and set her cup back in its blue saucer. "Life was slower and more elegant, but there were more rules. I was carefully taught to be a lady. Every night Papa would choose either me or my sister to be his hostess for the dinner meal. We would have to sit opposite him, formally dressed, never letting our backs touch the backs of our chairs. We had to converse with the adults present, sometimes for hours, no matter how tedious we found the conversation. We had to practice entering the dining room and leaving it, pouring the tea or coffee, again and again until he was satisfied with our performance. I tried to teach you all these things..." Her faint voice trailed away. "But times change. You would never sit still."

"I remember those lessons," Noelle said fondly. "You were very determined. I was such a failure."

"You were too much like your mama."

"I..."

"Don't take offense, child. Your mama has a charm and a vitality that great ladies all too often lack. She's made Wade very happy."

"I never heard you compliment her before."

"I must be getting old." Marlea smiled. "But she was kind to me after the stroke when I could barely speak and you were away. Maybe she always was, but I was too strong and too stubbornly against what I considered Wade's misalliance to notice before.''

Noelle almost felt that she could have brought up the subject of Garret and *Grand-mère* might have tried to understand.

Noelle knotted her hands together and lapsed into silence. Garret had been busy lately. With Carnival, and the additional police work it involved, he'd been too busy to resolve any of their problems. When he wasn't working overtime for the police department, he was at Mannie's helping his mother with the extra customers the season always brought. Noelle had hardly seen him. Not that she hadn't been busy herself in her shop. But without Garret she'd been aware of the season rushing past her, of the balls that she wasn't going to, of the life she'd given up for a man who suddenly had so little time for her. Beau had come by the shop once and told her about a particularly spectacular ball she had missed. Afterward, when Garret had not even called her that evening, she'd become even more restless than before. She kept wondering if he was deliberately avoiding her. So when *Grand-mère* had said she was going to Martin House to get away from all the excitement and the crowds, Noelle had offered to accompany her.

She'd wanted to think, away from Garret, away from the hubbub of Carnival. She had thought maybe she'd find the right moment to confide in *Grand-mère*.

The wind gusted colder and stronger. Noelle reached for the coffeepot and realized she needed to take it into the kitchen and rewarm it.

A few minutes later, Noelle was at the microwave when she glanced out the window and saw that *Grand-mère*'s rocker was rocking itself silently in the wind. Noelle dropped her pot holders and ran closer to the window.

Mon Dieu! Her grandmother was struggling with her cane to take shaky steps along the uneven brick walk to their dock at the bayou. The wind was swirling her black skirt around her frail body and tearing thin strands of silver hair loose from her bun. Beyond her grandmother, Noelle saw a slim boy fighting frantically to tie his pirogue to the dock before the wind swept him away and swamped the tiny craft. Water was inside the boat, curling around his ankles.

"Louis!"

Why hadn't *Grand-mère* called her? Noelle was out the door within seconds, shouting to them both as she raced past *Grand-mère* to the dock and caught Louis's line just as his boat was being carried away. She looped the line around a piling and tied it snugly and then pulled the tiny pirogue to shore.

When the boat was secure, Louis picked up a wild-eyed Carlotta and heaved the dog onto the dock and then jumped off himself. He threw a second line from the stern and tied it.

Noelle reached for the boy, pulled him to her and clung to him.

"Don't you know you shouldn't be out on a day like this," Noelle murmured, ruffling his hair, pressing her forehead to his.

He clung to her wordlessly, his slim arms wrapped around her neck, letting her pet him a minute more as the fierce wind gusted around them. Then something behind her caught his attention and he tugged free and dashed past her toward the house. Bereft, Noelle turned and saw that *Grand-mère* had dropped her cane and was struggling to lean down and retrieve it from the high grasses beside the bricks.

Louis reached her, picked up the cane and handed it to her. For a long time the old lady and the boy stared at each other speculatively. He with his big, silent, shy eyes; she with her sharp dark ones.

Noelle walked toward them slowly. Carlotta was already lying on the veranda wagging her sodden tail as if she had no doubt about her welcome.

"This is Garret's child, *Grand-mère*. His name is Louis."

Dubious blue eyes were still studying Marlea.

"I know who he is," *Grand-mère* said, but in her kindest, gentlest voice.

"He doesn't speak, *Grand-mère*."

"I know. But I'll bet he likes cookies."

Louis nodded warily, still shy and unsure.

Grand-mère took his hand. "You must come up to the house and sit with me while Noelle fixes us a plate of cookies and some tea."

While they were eating, it began to rain, hard at first. Then it slackened to a slow but steady downpour before stopping altogether. Noelle called Louis's grandmother and told her where he was.

After having cookies, Louis stayed to draw and then lingered on for sandwiches. Noelle found some crayons and paper, and Louis happily drew sketches of parade floats. Noelle asked him if he'd ever been to a parade and he shook his head, so she assumed he'd seen the floats on television. *Grand-mère* admired his pictures and began to talk of Mardi Gras, of the parades she had gone to as a child, of the costumes she had worn. Louis listened to everything she said, entranced, but silent.

"Louis, do you know that *Grand-mère*'s costumes are still in the attic," Noelle began.

His blue eyes were immense with excitement as he glanced up.

"We could go up there and try them on," Noelle offered softly.

He looked doubtfully at Carlotta who had polished off a tray of cookies herself and now lay thumping her tail at Marlea's feet.

"Carlotta will be fine. *Grand-mère* needs a friend to keep her company."

Very slowly Louis got up and came to Noelle. He studied her for a long moment and then threaded his fingers into hers.

Dressed in a sash and pirate costume, Louis leaped from an ancient Vuitton trunk. No longer was he the serious child who had been coloring quietly on the veranda.

He swung his imaginary sword at an imaginary foe. Beside him in the attic Noelle was digging through the contents of a second dusty trunk. She pulled out a roll of red velvet, which she draped around herself. Then she became aware of Louis who had stopped his play and pulled something else out of the trunk. It was a dress, made of topaz-colored velvet. He handed it to her and gestured for her to slip it on.

"I—I can't, Louis. It's been in the trunk for years and years. It's musty."

His silent eyes implored her, so that at last she relented and slipped it over her clothes. His eyes glowed with appreciation as he led her to a mottled mirror in the far corner of the attic near a dormer window.

As she studied her reflection, she was still buttoning tiny buttons up the front of the bodice. The skirt was so full—there were yards and yards of golden satin and velvet; it would need hoops, but the color brought out the whiskey gold of her eyes and transformed her into a beauty of another age.

She winked at Louis. "All I need is a mask and I will be the perfect lady to be courted by a ferocious pirate such as yourself."

Louis laughed, dazzled.

She thought of Garret. He would be furious at her.

She stroked Louis's hair. Across the room she saw their poignant reflection in the mirror. She lowered her cheek to the shimmering gold of his head. Garret wanted her to have nothing to do with his son. Noelle closed her eyes to shut out the pain of that thought as she hugged Garret's child.

"Tonight, if it stops raining, there's going to be a parade in New Orleans," she whispered. "Would you like to go?"

Louis nodded.

"I'd take you if you think your grandmother would let you go."

Louis's eyes were grave and yet shining with joy. Very carefully his mouth formed the soundless words, "I love you."

Noelle was filled with unbearable happiness. Suddenly she was as unable to speak as he. All she could do was pull him to her again and hold him tightly as tears squeezed through her lashes and rained down on the silky gold of his hair.

He was Garret's son. She had always loved him as if he were hers, too.

And loving him somehow helped make up for the baby she'd lost.

Ten

Garret's truck was partially off the road, hidden in the darkness of the trees. He sat in grim silence behind the wheel, waiting, a hot swift current running through him.

The parade had been over for hours. Where the hell were they?

Just as he asked himself this question for the hundredth time, he saw twin cones of light bobbing off the dark trees, vanishing, and then bobbing again as Noelle's Mercedes drew up to the small house dwarfed on all sides by cypress and pine.

Noelle alighted from her car, and Garret leaned forward, his body suddenly as taut as a bowstring. Silhouetted against the porch light in her gown of golden satin and velvet, she seemed a fantasy from the Old South as she circled the hood to help Louis out. Louis was masked as a diminutive pirate with a patch over one eye, and he was struggling manfully to hold a dozen plastic necklaces and handfuls of Carnival doubloons.

Suddenly everything in his arms spilled to the ground, and both Louis and Noelle knelt to retrieve it. Afterward as she handed him the last doubloon, she hugged him tenderly for a long moment as if he were very precious to her.

Garret's brows knotted in a deep frown as he observed the clinging pair. Louis's face was aglow, his eyes shining with timid adoration.

Garret was furious. But he was dazzled, too, as dazzled as his son, by some soft secret, a long-desired emotion that threatened to overflow inside him and leave him totally vulnerable. He clutched the steering wheel so tightly his knuckles turned white.

Garret loved her, yet he almost hated her for doing this to him. Just as Louis wanted to be part of a family, Garret wanted a family, as well—to be both father and husband again. But he was afraid. Bone-deep afraid of Noelle. Afraid of trusting her. Afraid of losing everything all over again. He had tried to pretend that more than anything he was afraid for Louis, but it wasn't true. He was afraid for himself. Selfishly, stupidly afraid.

He had so many memories. For many years he had fought to forget. He had left Louis with Annie's mother so he wouldn't see his own pain reflected daily in his son's eyes.

Memories came back to Garret in a dark flicker of images. Noelle and he making love beneath sunlight and shadows when they were young along the bayou's edge. Noelle gone, and the emptiness he'd felt every time he'd gone there without her. The years of loneliness. Annie...their marriage...her death...the guilt and agony afterward. And then Noelle again...and that terrible final night when their baby had died and she'd nearly died, as well. He'd blamed himself for that, too, but he'd buried the blame. If he'd only listened when she'd tried to explain about Raoul... Louis's silent shock when Noelle did not return. Garret's own guilt made stronger knowing that he was the cause of his son's misery.

Garret had told himself he was through, finished with love and commitment, but Noelle was back in his life. And everything was starting again. Every day he could feel himself caring more for her. She made him laugh, she made him feel alive again.

Garret had tried to avoid her for the past two weeks, tried to forget her, but he hadn't been able to help himself. He was in the grip of something too strong to break. And now she was involving Louis.

Damn her. He should have known she would try something like this. She had said she was coming to Martin House to accompany her grandmother who wanted to get away from the Mardi Gras crowds. And he'd been glad— glad to be rid of her—although in the end it hadn't helped. Her absence had only made him realize how hopelessly he was obsessed.

Had she deliberately lied to him? Had she thought herself safe, that he was trapped in the city by the long hours he had to work, that he would never find out what she was really up to? Hadn't she realized that he always called to check on Louis, that he would discover that she had taken him into the city for the Momus parade? Annie's mother had tried to explain—something about Noelle rescuing Louis and Louis being almost happy for the first time since Noelle had gone out of his life two years before—but Garret had cut her short and driven out to wait for Noelle instead.

Noelle vanished inside the front door, and Garret got out of his truck and walked up to the porch. She stayed inside only a minute, but as he stood in the dark and studied the golden sliver of light beneath the door, he caught fragments of her gentle goodbyes. Through the window he could see Louis holding her, not letting her go until she promised to come by the next day. And the sight of them together awakened in Garret a longing so intense he wanted to smash something to obliterate it.

When she came outside again, the porch light turned her hair to flame. Despite his anger and confusion Garret was piercingly aware of how lovely she was. Her tight bodice and hooped skirts made her figure look like an hourglass. Yellow lace frothed at her bosom. She wore a yellow ribbon in her hair. He inhaled the scent of wild roses.

All week he had thought of her constantly. Now that she was near, his need of her throbbed like a fever in his blood.

He wanted her. He hated her. He loved her.

"Chère..."

When she saw him standing in the shadows, she almost cried out. He moved toward her silently and grabbed her, pulling her out into the darkness away from the lighted house.

"Garret, please don't hurt me."

She was soft and warm—beautiful, desirable. The deafening roar of his own heart seemed to pound against his eardrums.

He clasped her captured wrist, holding it hard when she would have drawn it loose. "You lied to me, *chère*."

"No."

"You said you wanted to be with your grandmother."

"I did. Louis came over—"

"I don't want to hear any of it! Do you understand?" And yet he did. He wanted to believe every tender word of defense she uttered, and that made him even angrier. "All I know is that you came here and deliberately defied me by taking Louis to New Orleans to see that parade."

"He wanted to go! It's wrong of you to bury him out here! He's a little boy!"

"*My* little boy."

"He could have been... ours. I want so much... to be a mother to him... Oh, Garret..."

Pain twisted Garret's heart. "I told you to stay away from him."

"He'd never even seen a parade. You should have seen how happy he was there."

Garret was miserable, torn. Neither Noelle nor Garret heard the back door open. Nor did they notice the sliver of light widen as a tiny figure slipped outside and stealthily approached them.

"Garret, please..."

Garret felt himself weakening, but he told himself he had to be strong—for Louis's sake. "Stay away from Louis!"

"I love him! And he loves—"

Ruthlessly Garret snapped her slim body even closer to his own. "His love for you flatters you. That's all."

"No..."

She was struggling to free herself, but he was too strong. His fingers wound through her hair to still her head. Her red hair was shaken loose from its ribbon and tumbled down her shoulders.

"Daddy..."

The whispered word from behind them was a shock to Garret's nervous system. He whirled and saw his son standing in the darkness. Garret could only stare in frozen wonder as the little boy leaned down and picked up the yellow ribbon. It was a long time before Garret himself was able to speak.

"Louis, you talked. You actually spoke," Garret managed huskily.

"Don't hurt her, Dad." Then Louis ran to Noelle and threw his arms around her as she slowly knelt to his level and took her ribbon back. "And please, please don't make her go away again."

"Darling, Louis," she said quietly, pressing him close. "Darling, darling..." From beneath lowered lashes she glanced up at Garret, her own eyes radiant until she met his cold black gaze.

Numbly Garret sank to his knees beside them. Just as numbly he was aware of Noelle rising, of her gently placing his son in his arms and then retreating to the shadows behind them so that father and son could be alone.

As he hugged his child, it was one of the most wonderful moments in Garret's life. Louis *had* spoken!

Garret glanced past his son and saw the desolation in Noelle's eyes.

He clenched his hands into fists and pressed them against his thighs.

And then he knew that it was one of the most terrible moments.

Didn't she know that she was tearing him to pieces?

Garret opened his liquor cabinet and splashed Scotch into a single glass. Noelle was in his living room behind him, but he didn't invite her to join him. It had been a long day—eighteen hours long. Then there had been the hours in the truck waiting for her, followed by the scene with Louis.

Garret drank the liquor in a single swallow, letting it burn all the way down his throat, willing it to burn away the emotions that consumed him. Then he poured another.

"Garret why did you want me to follow you here if you're just going to ignore me and drink?"

The glass hit the counter violently, and liquor spilled over his tanned hand onto the table top.

There was a smoldering silence. He turned slowly and regarded her in the dim lamplight.

She looked different in the golden velvet dress. The color made her eyes look like fire or maybe her eyes would have blazed just as fiercely anyway. He didn't know. He didn't care. His own feelings were equally powerful.

"Because I want to settle this issue about Louis once and for all."

"So do I."

Garret picked up the glass and downed the remaining liquid, again in a single swallow. "You want it all, don't you? Me? My son? Everything?"

"Is that so wrong?"

"It always has been in the past. You destroyed me... Louis... I can't forget that, Noelle."

"You won't even try."

"Because you don't even try to live up to a single promise. You swore you'd stay away from him."

"And I did."

"No."

"Garret, he came to me. Twice. I can't turn my back on him again. It would be like rejecting my own child. I lost my baby. Our baby. That's something I'll never get over."

"Shut up about the baby."

In a fury of frustration he reached for the bottle again. Noelle crossed the room and took his arm before he could touch it. "Don't—"

There was an electricity that went from her skin to his the second she touched him. It was like a shock burning the length of his body.

"I love you," she said. "I want you. And I want your child. I said before...that he could have been ours. Sometimes...I almost feel that he is...my son."

Garret jerked free of her and clenched his hand into a ball and unclenched it. "But do you really? Or are you still the rich fickle Martin girl, bored by your easy life, who'll go running off to Australia or Europe or with Vincent or somebody else that's as rich or richer than he is whenever it suits you?"

"When are you ever going to realize I was never that girl?" she asked hopelessly, even as she was touching him with her hands and kissing him with her lips.

"Don't to that, *chère*—"

"Don't do what?" she purred, lifting her head, peering at him with those gorgeous eyes that bathed his face with golden heat.

Her fingertips were hot seductive velvet. His hand closed over hers. "I don't want to be a toy you play with when you're in between rich lovers."

"You aren't."

"Don't forget, *chère*, I've read every story ever written about you in the society columns." His voice was softly ominous.

"Every one of them was for *Grand-mère* and Papa. Those parties and stories were things I felt I was forced to do. I always felt bored and restless—so lonely. Those people paid attention to me because I was a Martin, not because I was me."

"Go home, *chère*—"

"I would if I could live without you, Garret."

Her hands were against his thigh. His skin became flame. And she was flame.

If he had a grain of sense he would throw her out. She was a Martin, and he'd never had much luck with Martins.

But the flame was inside him, devouring him. There was confusion in his heart, but part of the confusion was a love so intense he couldn't ignore it. He could no more do without her than he could do without the air he breathed. His lips were on hers, and his hands began to rip the tiny buttons of her bodice apart.

He wanted her, and this wildness to have her was like nothing he had ever felt for another woman. His hands were shaking like a boy's as he caressed her breasts.

He knew that this woman could probably never be true to him or to Louis, but as long as he could have her, he would.

With an eagerness he could no longer restrain he lifted her into his arms and carried her into the bedroom.

He forgot his exhaustion and made love to her for hours. She was as insatiable as he.

But if she thought Louis was an argument that she could win in bed, she was wrong.

Afterward, when it was nearly dawn, Garret said, "You can't imagine what Louis was like after Annie died. And then again after you left him.... Stay away from Louis, *chère*. Or we're through."

Outside, creepers of rosy light were shining through the black trees.

But the icy darkness in the bedroom was like a wall that crushed down upon them both.

In that cold darkness Noelle got up and dressed quietly.

In that darkness she walked quickly out of Garret's house.

In that darkness he listened to the purr of her diesel engine when she started her car in his drive.

Noelle stood beneath the shelter of the veranda, shivering as she sipped a cup of tea. Rain was pouring from the gutters of Martin House. Beyond the bayou was darkly forbidding. For the past two days it had been raining, ever since that night Noelle had last seen Garret. In New Orleans several parades had been canceled. Mardi Gras itself was in jeopardy.

At least the rain meant that Louis couldn't come to Martin House, and she hadn't been faced with the decision of rejecting him if he defied Garret. No sooner had she thought this than she saw a slim shape moving on the bayou through the rain.

"Mon Dieu!"

Noelle's teacup clattered when she replaced it in its saucer. She could hardly believe her eyes as she recognized boy and boat.

Louis was poling his pirogue steadily toward the dock through the driving rain.

She dashed out into the rain; in seconds she was soaked through. The bayou was so swollen that the water was lapping over the dock.

For a moment both boy and woman stood in the rain, staring at each other, hesitating. His eyes were big and blue and desolate, as desolate as her own. He was disobeying his father to come to her.

She loved Garret, yet she knew that by loving his child, she was risking everything. Still, Louis was only six. He'd watched his mother die violently. Since then he'd lived apart from his father. Louis was reaching out to her.

She thought of the two long years in Australia when she'd tried to forget her own tragedies. Louis was a child. He hadn't been able to run away. Perhaps she was his salvation. Perhaps he was hers.

He smiled crookedly, charmingly, and she could resist no longer. She pulled him from the pirogue into her arms. Together they raced to the house where she took him into the bathroom, pulling off his wet clothes while he shivered, wrapping him in thick Turkish towels while she dried his clothes in the dryer. She changed her own clothes. *Grand-mère* came down, and the three of them had tea on the veranda. Noelle was aware of *Grand-mère* watching her when she was with Louis with a much keener interest than usual.

Louis stayed for lunch and the rest of the afternoon, leaving when there was a lull in the weather just before sundown.

After he had gone, Marlea shakily followed Noelle into her bedroom. Marlea was feeble, but her mottled, wise old eyes saw deeply and clearly. "It's quite hopeless this time, I suppose?" she said raspily in her ancient, beloved voice.

She had caught Noelle completely unawares.

"What?"

"Your love for the boy's father—that Garret Cagan?"

Marlea hobbled toward the rosewood bed and fussed with a lace coverlet. Noelle watched her, relief flooding her as she realized her grandmother was not reproaching her but had accepted this reality. No explanations were being asked.

"Quite . . . hopeless," Noelle answered with as much dignity as possible.

"I told you he'd make you unhappy," *Grand-mère* said a bit smugly, leaning on her cane.

"He wants me to stay away from Louis."

"That poor motherless child needs you. What are you going to do? Knuckle under spinelessly or fight?"

"I don't know."

"No matter what else happens, never forget that you're a Martin."

Noelle felt her grandmother's strength of will pouring into her in a warm powerful tide of love. Noelle had come to her room in defeat, not knowing what to do.

"You'll have to fight," Marlea said, taking Noelle's young smooth hands in her old gnarled ones. "Garret Cagan's as stubborn as they come. I don't believe I ever saw anyone struggle harder to get somewhere in this world than that boy. I thought he was a gold digger, but there's more to him than that."

"Thank you, *Grand-mère*."

It seemed a miracle that at last her grandmother understood and supported her.

Louis came the next day again, and the next. Noelle could not turn him away even though she knew that she was risking her relationship with Garret by not doing so.

On Mardi Gras it was still raining, but lightly as Noelle drove up to Annie's mother's house. Noelle jumped out of the car and ran up the wooden stairs. Before she could even knock, the door opened.

Louis's grandmother stood there in a white apron, holding a dish towel.

Usually Louis was first to the door. Noelle felt a vague unease.

"Where's Louis, Analise?"

There was sudden alarm on the woman's broad, kindly face. "I thought he was with you. He said you were coming around ten."

Noelle felt panic welling up in her. "I'm running nearly an hour late. Eva called about the business."

"He came into the kitchen. It must have been a little after ten. He said something about you. I was baking. I assumed you'd come for him in your car."

Without another word both women ran down the stairs toward the bayou only to discover that his pirogue was gone.

"I told him the bayou was flooding and not to take the pirogue again," Analise whispered frantically as she stared at the empty dock. "Usually he minds me."

"I'll go look for him at Martin House."

But he wasn't there.

And when Noelle called Analise, she discovered that he hadn't returned home, either.

The sky darkened, and the rain began to fall more thickly. A wild, furious wind roared through the trees. Noelle turned on the television and learned that the bayous were already out of their banks. The river was swelling, and the levee was weakening in several places. A dangerous weather system was moving swiftly into the area. There were flash-flood warnings. If the levee went, the low swamplands would be completely flooded.

Noelle glanced out the window. Lightning set the entire sky aflame. Then a bolt exploded right outside the house.

There was a rending crash. The world shuddered as a giant live oak split and fell to the ground, taking the power cables with it.

The room melted into darkness. The television set went black.

Noelle went to the window and watched with numb horror as the storm moved in.

Marlea hobbled shakily into the living room. "There you are..."

"*Grand-mère*, Louis is out in the swamp! Alone! He's probably in trouble. I have to find him. Call Garret. Oh, please. Tell him that I'm sorry, that I love him, that he has to come... Oh, *Grand-mère*... in case I fail..."

"Wait, *chère*!"

But Noelle was already running out of the room.

One thing Garret knew—Mrs. Martin would never call him unless she was completely desperate.

He rolled up the windows of his truck and pressed the receiver of his portable phone closer to his ear. He could hardly hear the frail elderly voice above the shouts of the Mardi Gras crowd. Despite the black clouds hovering above the city, Rex had left his den, and his subjects thronged both sides of Canal Street.

"I said your boy's lost in the swamp, and my Noelle's gone to find him."

Garret's blood seemed to freeze solid. His entire being became icy and terrified. "You're telling me that there's a violent storm and that they're both out there in it?"

The crowd roared again. Another float, no doubt, passing by.

Damn! He couldn't hear a thing.

"Could you speak a little louder, Mrs. Martin?"

"Two years ago when I nearly lost Noelle... I—I—"

Hell, he didn't want to be reminded of that. But he heard her fear, as great as his own, and his heart filled with unwanted compassion. It didn't matter that she'd always been against him.

"Mrs. Martin, don't you worry, no. I'll get there just as fast as I can."

Before his pager had gone off, Garret had been trying to settle a fight that had erupted between a pair of drunken maskers waiting for Rex and his parade—an Arab and a potbellied bumblebee. Johnson had been cuffing the bumblebee while Garret had gone to his truck to phone in.

Mrs. Martin continued speaking, but as hard as Garret strained to hear her, he couldn't quite make out her words.

"I'm coming, Mrs. Martin. I'm coming," he yelled before hanging up on her.

He whipped out his portable light and clamped it onto the roof of his truck. He turned on his siren, backed down an alley and then rushed down a narrow side street that led away from the parade and the crowds. He radioed the dispatcher and told her to notify Johnson that he was on his own.

A child ran into the street. Garret hit his brakes and swerved. His truck careened into a pair of garbage cans and sent them bouncing into a brick wall, but the child scampered to safety.

Damn!

Noelle!

Always Noelle! Always testing his love for her in some wild defiance of fate! But this was worse because Louis was involved.

She never gave a damn about what he, Garret, wanted, only about what she wanted. If he got Louis and her out of this one alive, he really was through with her.

This time for good.

If...

The truck jounced into a pothole and Garret's teeth bit into his tongue so hard he tasted the bitter flavor of his own blood.

If...

It wasn't much past noon, but it was as dark as dusk when Garret's truck swerved into the driveway that curved through the familiar tunnel of perpetual twilight that held the promise of glimmering white columns at its end.

It hadn't been raining in the city, but it was falling in sheets so thickly here that he'd barely been able to see to drive the last twenty miles.

There were lights in only one room of Martin House. Garret could hear the thunder of a generator as he ran up the brick walk to the house.

The hand-carved door stood ajar. He ran through it without knocking. The old lady was just inside, sitting in the dark on her rosewood sofa, waiting for him.

Her raspy voice came from the corner. "Garret..."

She struggled to get up, but she was thin and weak and shaking even more than usual because of her fear.

He went to her and lifted her gently, steadying her. He reached for her cane, but she clung to him instead.

"You have a fine boy."

"He's like his mother."

"He's like you, too. I was wrong about you," she said.

Her hands holding on to him felt like claws.

"Tell me everything, Mrs. Martin."

"Louis's pirogue was missing. We think he was trying to pole his way over here, but he never made it. Noelle took her pirogue to look for him."

"She what! That leaky thing has been in the boat house for years!"

"It was all we had."

"If they'd stayed apart the way I told them to, none of this would have ever happened. The levee could go at any minute. Then everything out there will be under ten feet of water."

Garret was about to go.

"Garret—"

Despite his urgent desire to leave, something in her deadly quiet voice stopped him.

"Noelle wanted you that night. She kept calling for you even when we thought she was dying. She wanted your baby."

"But you told me..."

Heartbreak and weariness possessed the frail old woman, and she dropped her head in her hands and wept in despair. "I had raised her. She was my child. I thought I knew what was best for her."

He drew a deep breath. "I wasn't good enough."

"I'm an old woman, used to the old ways." Her swollen red eyes met his, naked and pleading. "I don't deserve your forgiveness, Garret."

"And I don't deserve Noelle's. You see, I believed you."

His face hard, he stared down at Marlea without the slightest intention of forgiving her. She had always been his nemesis. She'd been against him for as long as he could remember—even when he'd been a child. For years he had hated her. She had heartlessly thrown his mother and him out. Just as heartlessly she had made him believe that Noelle was glad that their baby had died.

But the old lady was crying now, and he had never seen her cry. He had never thought that women of her strong character had tears, and a flood of unwanted tenderness swept through him. For the first time he saw Mrs. Martin as the frail human creature she was—a spoiled old matriarch, fragile, terrified by her failing powers and the changing world, but courageous as well.

Because of this old lady, he had hated all the Martins. He had never been able to trust Noelle. For years he had lived on this hatred, thrived on it. Indeed, everything he had ever achieved had been through that single emotion. Hatred had been the secret of the ambition that had driven him constantly to prove himself.

He thought of Noelle and Louis, how Noelle had fought to change his mind about the kind of person she was. She had wanted his baby! She had wanted him! But he had refused to believe in her!

She was out there, risking her own life to save his son.

Never had he known the depth of his love for her until that moment when he felt he might lose her forever. In that instant he knew that hatred had served its purpose in his life.

Gradually his hard face softened and he patted Marlea's thin arm as though he were comforting a child. Her hand closed around his, and for a long moment he stood there and let her cling.

Then he turned on his heel and was gone.

The rain that pounded into Garret's eyes felt as cold and sharp as slivers of sleet. Recklessly he drove the airboat through the swamp beneath the dark trees. The flat-bottomed boat left the green-black water and flew over a grassy patch. The airboat hit smooth water again with a violent thud.

On and on he raced, through a never-ending, verdant canopy of trees, down a series of canals and dead-end waterways, into blind lakes. On and on, but always without success.

It seemed that the whole world had become rain and wet trees and dark water, that there could be no place that was not flooded.

If the river itself flooded, if the levees gave way...

He would not think of that.

As he raced along he was not conscious of the passing of time. Only of the urgency of his search. He had to find them, before it was too late.

A log loomed out of the bayou, and Garret swerved the airboat.

But not in time.

The edge of the boat hit a tangle of roots and trunk. The airboat went flying again, but not in the direction Garret was steering. Instead it flipped and careened crazily toward a wall of trees. Just at the last moment before the boat hull smashed into the tree trunks, Garret was hurled free—toward the soft black muddy bank.

Garret had heard it said that right before a man dies, his whole life passes in front of him. In those last fleeting seconds Garret thought only of Noelle. He saw her sweet face, framed by the wild red tumble of her hair. He remembered how her body had quivered beneath his hands. He'd hurt her by refusing to believe in her, to trust her. In agony Garret remembered how she'd dressed in the darkness of his room that last morning, how she'd stumbled from his house. How he'd lain there like the cold, heartless bastard he was and stubbornly refused to call her back. All these things he remembered in the flash of those last seconds.

He had never told her he still loved her.

He hadn't wanted to believe it.

If he died, she'd never know.

His body smashed into the soft bank, but his head hit wood.

The world went black.

Eleven

***

Garret's lashes fluttered. A dazzling light hurt his eyes and behind the light there was flame. The right side of his skull throbbed.

Heaven or hell? Where was he?

He closed his eyes again, not really caring. All he knew was that he was lying on a soft bed in a dark room.

A tart voice broke through his dazed senses.

"Some hero! What's the world coming to when a helpless Southern belle has to get herself all wet and muddy and do the rescuing?"

"Noelle!"

Garret tried to sit up. The right side of his head felt as though it had been pounded with a brick. Movement produced pain but so did staying still. So he continued struggling until he was upright.

"Who did you think it was?" her gently mocking voice demanded.

He opened his eyes to the glory of her beauty. He saw the tears on her lashes. Suddenly he felt a searing joy to have found her again, to know that she must still care for him.

"An angel or a devil—I wasn't sure." His voice was soft and shook with an emotion he no longer made any attempt to conceal. "But then I never am with you. Noelle... *chère*...I was so wrong... So..." A huge knot in his throat made it impossible for him to go on.

"Don't you remember anything?" she asked gravely.

Vaguely he remembered awakening on that muddy bank and finding her there in the rain beside him. She had helped him up. Together they had struggled through the mud and palmetto fronds with him stumbling and leaning heavily upon her.

He felt her fingertips smooth his hair from his injured temple, and he closed his eyes to save the light sweetness of that gesture. "I guess I thought I was dreaming," he whispered. "I don't deserve you. I—"

"Hush... You're in the houseboat," she said. "The rain stopped yesterday. I radioed *Grand-mère* that we're okay. She'll send a boat as soon as she can."

"Yesterday?" He'd lost a whole day. "Where's Louis?"

"Right here, Dad."

Louis hopped onto the bed, jouncing the mattress ever so lightly, but every move felt as if a knife were stabbing Garret's temple. The sound of Louis's voice, though, and his smile of utter joy made up for the pain.

Garret grabbed his son and held him close. He felt the frail, slim child, plunged his callused hand through his thick golden hair. Then he pushed Louis away so that he could study his sweet smile and lovely big eyes. "Dear God, you're okay. You're both okay."

"I was coming to see Noelle, Dad, 'cause I thought she forgot to pick me up. Only a gator slapped his tail on a log and scared me so bad I fell out of the pirogue. I broke my pole, and the wind started blowing my boat around. Noelle found me, though, and brought me here.''

Noelle started to back away and leave them together, but Garret touched her hand. The thought of them being a family scared him, but it scared him more to think of losing either one of them.

Gently she slipped her fingers through his and held on to him tightly. He felt a suddenly overwhelming burst of happiness as he pulled her down on top of them.

''No...you're not getting away that easily, *chère*. Never again.'' Possessively he stroked her warm wrist.

''What?''

''I mean I want you both, forever,'' he whispered huskily. ''Always.''

''Really, Dad?''

''Be quiet, Louis, so I can ask this lady to marry me.''

Louis's eyes widened in astonishment. But he obeyed instantly, watching his smiling father and Noelle, his slim face aglow. Then he winked at his father. ''I think I'll take my fishing pole outside for a little while.''

''Good idea, son.''

There were tears of happiness in Noelle's eyes again as she watched Louis disappear out the door. ''Garret, I thought you'd be furious,'' she said in a soft tone, as dazed and dazzled as Louis. ''You told me never to see Louis again.''

''I was wrong about that, so wrong. Louis needs you just as I need you, but I couldn't let myself believe in you. It was my fault you left Louis in the first place two years ago. My fault because I was too jealous to listen to you. I drove you away to Australia because I believed my own doubts and an old woman's lies. If I'd had a grain of sense I'd have followed you to the end of the world and begged you to come back to me. I've been a fool, *chère*. We lost our baby, you nearly died—because of me."

"It was an accident," she said in her gentlest tone. "An unfortunate accident."

"No. Everything that happened was my fault, and I made it all worse by being so hard on you. I made you endure it alone. I'll have to live with that for the rest of my life. Then I kept you from Louis—to protect him I said. But that was a lie. I was afraid to admit how much I loved you. I was afraid of losing you all over again."

He placed his hand on the side of her cheek, and she leaned closer and kissed him softly on the lips, moving her mouth against his with subtle seductive movements until she felt his hands tighten around her.

"Oh, Garret," she murmured. "You really want to marry me? You really love me?"

"I've always loved you, *chère*. Since we were kids. There's never been anyone to compare with you. Only I didn't think you'd have me."

He kissed her again, his lips warm and tender as they clung together.

She pulled away and laughed shakily. "You're sure you don't just want someone around to match your ties?"

"Very sure."

Garret touched her hair, wound his fingers through two thick coils of coppery silk. "Did I ever tell you how much I love your red hair?"

Her smile was radiant. "Really? Do you mean it?"

"*Chère*, what I want more than anything is for Louis to have a little sister who has beautiful red hair...just like yours."

"Oh, Garret." Noelle melted into his arms once more.

He caught the scent of wild roses.

"I feel like I've been waiting for this moment all my life."
His mouth closed over hers hungrily.

"If you don't stop, we may end up with a whole houseful of redheads."

"*Chère*, I'm not going to stop, no. Not ever."

"Louis is just outside."

"Our child," he whispered, lifting her hair and lacing soft warm kisses along her nape.

"Ours?"

"Ours." He murmured. "Everything I possess—my heart, my soul, my child—are yours. Forever."

Garret wrapped his arms around her, and she nestled close to him. Outside they could hear Louis singing as he threw out a fishing line. Louis, happy at last, singing with joy like any normal kid. Garret's arms tightened around Noelle. She had given him back his son.

The air was fresh and rain scented. It was a new morning, a morning that held the promise of new life, of mingled futures that would be long and happy.

Garret bent his head and kissed Noelle, softly at first, but soon he could no longer hold back.

"My love," he whispered. "My love."

* * * * *

Silhouette Sensation

presents
THIS MAGIC MOMENT
by NORA ROBERTS

This classic love story, written by one of Silhouette's most popular and prolific authors, has now been made into a major television film, starring renowned actress Jenny Seagrove and Emmy-winner John Shea.

We are delighted to bring the original story to you as a very special September Silhouette Sensation novel featuring the stars of the film on the cover.

> *Pierce Atkins had thrilled audiences all over the world and, amid the glitter and glamour of Las Vegas, he enthralled Ryan Swan.*

> *Ryan saw that Pierce's past had taught him to rely on nothing. Could she really expect him to change?*

Don't forget, **This Magic Moment** is available next month from your regular Silhouette Sensation stockist. You won't want to miss it!

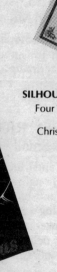
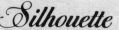

COMING NEXT MONTH

MIXED MESSAGES
Linda Lael Miller

Carly Barnett was determined to show Mark Holbrook that she was not just another blonde bimbo. Journalism was her dream and she knew that she was a talented writer. How was she going to get the top reporter to take her seriously?

WRONG ADDRESS, RIGHT PLACE
Lass Small

Linda Parsons hated lies and Mitch Roads had told her a real whopper. She thought she was the first customer of a small bed-and-breakfast place, when actually all Mitch was doing was renovating the house for his friends. How would she react when she found out he'd misled her deliberately so that they could get to know each other?

KISS ME KATE
Helen R. Myers

October's *Man of the Month*, Giles Channing, is British and he's also the kind of man who loves a challenge — especially one as irresistible as kissable Kate!

Silhouette Desire

COMING NEXT MONTH

TIME ENOUGH FOR LOVE
Carole Buck

Doug and Amy Browne had been the perfect
modern couple until their marriage buckled under
the strain of long periods apart. Doug was forced to
reassess his priorities and he decided to share his new
lifestyle with the only woman he'd ever loved. But
how was he going to persuade Amy?

BABE IN THE WOODS
Jackie Merritt

Eden knew she'd been stupid; she shouldn't have
come to Montana, she shouldn't have borrowed an
isolated cabin and, above all, she shouldn't have
accidentally shot Devlyn Stryker. Now she was
having to look after him and he was taking his
revenge, making it clear that he'd be happy to have
an affair!

TAKE THE RISK
Susan Meier

Caitlin Petrunak knew the type: rich, powerful and
manipulative. What would someone as wealthy as
Michael Flannery want with her?

VIDEO CAMCORDER COMPETITION
HOW TO ENTER

Listed below are the names of five actresses and their partners. To enter, simply match each couple by placing the letter in the box corresponding to the partner's name. For example if you think Joanne Woodward and Ryan O'Neil are a couple then place a B in the box next to Ryan O'Neil's name.

A Jerry Hall   Don Johnson   [ ]

B Joanne Woodward   Andrew Lloyd-Webber   [ ]

C Melanie Griffiths   Paul Newman   [ ]

D Farrah Fawcett   Mick Jagger   [ ]

E Sarah Brightman   Ryan O'Neil   [ ]

When you have filled each of the boxes above, please complete the following tie-breaker in no more than 12 words.

I think the most romantic couple is [   ] because . . . .

. . . .

NAME _____

ADDRESS _____

POSTCODE _____ COUNTRY _____

Closing Date: 31st January, 1991

PLEASE SEND YOUR COMPLETED ENTRY TO:
Silhouette Camcorder Competition, Eton House, 18-24 Paradise Road, Richmond, Surrey, England TW9 1SR
or Readers in Southern Africa to;
Silhouette Camcorder Competition, IBS Pty Limited, Private Bag X3010, Randburg 2125, S.A.

✂ —

RULES AND CONDITIONS
FOR THE COMPETITION AND FILM OFFER

Please retain this section